MY PRISONER AND OTHER STORIES

THE JOURNAL NON/FICTION PRIZE

MY PRISONER AND OTHER STORIES

TYLER McANDREW

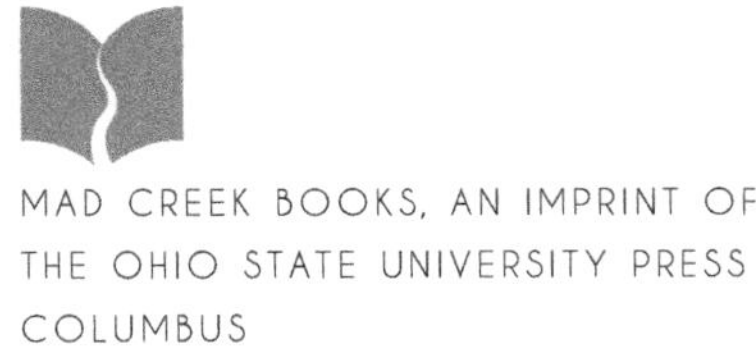

MAD CREEK BOOKS, AN IMPRINT OF
THE OHIO STATE UNIVERSITY PRESS
COLUMBUS

Library of Congress Cataloging-in-Publication Data
Names: McAndrew, Tyler author
Title: My prisoner and other stories / Tyler McAndrew.
Description: Columbus : Mad Creek Books, an imprint of The Ohio State University Press, 2025. | Summary: "A collection of stories about youth, loneliness, and coming to terms with the everyday and rippling violence of American life"— Provided by publisher.
Identifiers: LCCN 2025007729 | ISBN 9780814259511 paperback | ISBN 9780814284223 ebook
Subjects: LCGFT: Short stories
Classification: LCC PS3613.C2656 M9 2025 | DDC 813/.6—dc23/eng/20250318
LC record available at https://lccn.loc.gov/2025007729

Cover design by adam bohannon
Text design by Stuart Rodriguez
Type set in Caviar Dreams and Adobe Caslon Pro

For my mom and dad

CONTENTS

MY PRISONER

I was gathering sticks in the field when someone waved to me from a window of the state prison. It was early summer, crickets vibrating all around. The sky ripe with dusk. Against the stout concrete building, I could just make out the motion, a distance away, the arm extended from the tiny slit of a window, waving frantically. The sort of big, dramatic wave that you see people doing in old movies, like when lovers are departing on a train. I looked at the guard towers, the layers of fence crowned with barbed wire, the sign reading *STATE PRISON—NO TRESPASS-ING—Dept. of Corrections.* There was no one else nearby who the wave might have been intended for, so I waved back. In another moment, the floodlights clicked on and I shuffled back into the woods toward home.

The next day, the arm was there again, reaching out from between the bars and waving to me just as it had before. It was afternoon and I could see the whole thing more definitively, could see how excitedly the arm moved, back and forth, in a proud arc. The emotion of the gesture seemed unmistakable, as if the person on the other side of the bars was brimming with joy at the sight of me. This time, I couldn't help but feel excited too. I dropped my sticks and jumped in the air and waved my arms over my head like I was signaling a plane to the runway.

The prison stood in a long field surrounded by woods that eventually led back to my street and the house where I lived with my parents and older brother. I was building a fort in the woods. There was a fallen oak just past the edge of the field, and I stood in its ditch and wove sticks through the exposed roots to make a roof. My brother thought the fort was stupid, and he told me so every chance he got. But I had big plans. I imagined an elaborate series of treetop platforms connected by ropes and ladders and elevated boardwalks. All I'd managed so far, though, was a hole in the ground covered with an ugly mesh of roots and sticks.

The prisoner waved to me the next day, and the next day, and the next day after that. I worked on my fort each afternoon and then fell asleep each night wondering who the prisoner could be. I didn't know anyone in prison. I asked my brother, but he only laughed at me.

"I bet it's some psychopath," he said. "You know what? I bet it's that guy who kidnapped and murdered all those little kids a few years ago. Münz? Yeah, Münz the Maniac. That was his name."

What if it was Münz? Or some other monstrous criminal? I imagined serial killers with teeth like nails and cannibals dressed in blood-spattered aprons. The prisoner kept waving to me, every day, and at bedtime, my imagination unraveled like a scroll of every crime I'd ever heard of. What if it was a mafia hitman? What if it was the lady who had cut off her husband's penis? What if the arm belonged to some creep who drove a white van and diddled little kids?

But then I remembered the pictures I'd seen in school of Dr. Martin Luther King being led away in handcuffs. I decided the prisoner must be somehow noble or heroic. There was a boulder in the field outside the prison, and I made a habit of sitting down on it every afternoon while I was gathering sticks. I would sit on the rock and watch my prisoner waving, and I would wave back, and we would carry on that exchange, waving back and forth for a minute or two before I stood up and went back to building my fort. Once, I thought I heard him shouting something down to me—two syllables, unintelligible, the sound just barely discernible over the breeze. I stood still and listened, but the sound was too far away and could have come from anywhere.

I began to invent a whole life for my prisoner. After a few weeks, I came to the decision that he was a normal person who had simply been caught up in difficult circumstances. I decided that his crime was somehow righteous: he'd attacked his lover's abusive spouse or pulled a robbery to pay for his child's surgery. I imagined that he might be released some day, and not knowing where else to go, he might wait for me at the boulder in the field. I could shelter him in my fort, I thought, at least until he got back on his feet. I imagined sitting in my ditch, rain pittering on the roof I'd built, a column of smoke rising up through the trees as me and my prisoner cooked hot dogs over a fire. In another fantasy, I bumped into him somewhere—at the grocery store or the park—and recognized him simply by the energetic flap of his wave.

I held the prisoner in my imagination and every day, when I waved to him, my idea of him grew and became more whole. Maybe, I thought, the prisoner had, in fact, made serious mistakes. Mistakes for which his atonement must be profound. I came to the idea that he'd killed a pedestrian while driving drunk.

Or he'd been involved in gang violence at a young age and now, an adult, he'd been transformed by the weight of his guilt. In truth, I wanted for his crime to be both brutal and purposeful, a badge upon his soul that spoke to the absolute depths of his anguish and a testament to his reformation. Whoever the prisoner was, I just wanted to believe that he was a good person.

One night, I scrounged some cardboard from the recycling bin, and after everyone was asleep, I painted a sign. I wrote the word *Hi!* in dark blue letters, big enough to be read from a distance. When my brother found the sign the next day, he laughed at me. "You're really in love with the maniac, aren't you?" he said. "You're really in love with Münz. I bet if he ever gets out of that place, he's going to come straight here. First thing, he'll come looking for you." I didn't care. I marched out to the field and held up my sign. The prisoner waved to me with such joy, such enthusiasm. As if something great had happened. As if being here on Earth and being able to recognize another creature like yourself, if only from a distance, was cause enough for celebration.

Then, one day, late in the summer, I went out to gather sticks and was greeted only by the gray face of the prison building. I looked to the window and it was empty. I stood before the imposing shadow of the guard tower, the indifferent curl of barbed wire. I jogged the perimeter of the building, wondering if he had been moved to another cell. Maybe he had been released? A sick feeling began to form in my stomach. Maybe—oh, please, God, mercy—maybe he'd been given the death penalty?

I walked back into the woods and continued working on my fort but stopped when I noticed a pile of cigarette butts smashed up in the corner on the dirt floor. I stood for a moment in frozen panic, then noticed, tucked up among the roots of the fallen oak, a dirty magazine—a glossy pair of legs, opened wide, the pages wrinkled with moisture. Someone had been inside my fort. I remembered what my brother had said: if Münz was ever released, he'd come straight for me. Who else could it be? He'd seen me every day from the window of his cell, had seen me coming in and out of the woods. Anyone walking this direction from the prison would be able to find my dumb fort, no problem.

I yanked down the sticks that I'd so carefully woven until all that was left of my fort was a mess of dead branches scattered around the forest floor. I ran home and got there just in time for dinner. I ate silently, worrying that I'd left a trail—footprints or snapped twigs—that could be tracked back to my house.

But nothing happened. A few days later, I crept back through the woods. As I approached the site of my ruined fort, I could smell cigarettes. I hid behind an old log and watched from a distance as a figure stood up from the ditch of the fallen tree. My heart froze. But in a moment, I realized that it was just my brother. I watched him stub out a cigarette then wander off through the trees. I waited until he was out of sight. Then I walked out to the field and stared up at the empty window where there used to be a person who waved to me. I began to gather sticks.

THE FAMILIAR DARK

It was the time of year when people leave their windows open. Maria had burglarized three houses last week, just a few blocks from where she walked now, had slipped easily into darkened kitchens and dining rooms and taken small things—jewelry, liquor, cameras. Things that were easy to sell or that might not be immediately missed. In one house, she'd found a handgun, which she considered taking, but she got nervous. A theft like that, she thought, would demand attention, would be somehow easier to trace. She didn't think she could sell something like that at school and she didn't want to risk her foster parents finding it in their house. Maria was only fourteen and often scared more easily than she expected herself to.

It was about six o'clock in the evening. Cars pulling into driveways, parents coming home from work to greet their children. In another hour, the sun would go down and the neighborhood would settle, everyone sitting in front of their televisions, eating dinner, doing homework. Maria would walk slow loops between Barry Park and Euclid Avenue until most of the houses had lights on and then she would pick one of the few that stayed dark. The dark meant that no one was home, that she could go inside.

While she had stolen plenty in her life, burglary, for Maria, wasn't necessarily about the money. The state had taken her from her mother when she was young and in the shuffle of youth shelters and foster houses, she had never really known a place to feel like home. The closest she got to this feeling, she had discovered, was that sharp intimacy of being alone in someone else's house, touring their bedrooms and kitchens when they weren't there to guide her. She felt a sort of urgency when inspecting photographs of smiling strangers lining mantles or old receipts left on kitchen tables. She loved to look inside refrigerators and see what bizarre foods sustained a person, to peek into closets at whatever clutter they kept packed away, out of sight. There was a strange sensation—a delicate sadness and a greedy joy—in having her own little space, where she could imagine whatever life she wanted.

Maria was kneeling to tighten her shoelaces when she heard a voice, looked up, and saw an old woman standing in the lawn of a small brick house. The woman had tiny circular glasses and a cream-colored cardigan over an orange flower-print dress. She stood with hunched, broad shoulders and one hand raised, as if posing—a statue, waving hello.

"Excuse me," the old woman said, "can you help me?"

Maria finished tying her shoe and stood. "Is everything okay?" she asked.

"My husband," the old woman said. Her voice was small, but the words came blurting out with a sort of desperation. She opened her mouth, then closed it, as if she had forgotten what she was about to say. "I have locked myself out of the house," she began again. "My husband is away and will not be home until late. I was just moving some boxes from inside." She gestured toward the end of the driveway, where the garage door was rolled up on its track to reveal the cluttered interior: tool bench, wheelbarrow, rust-speckled refrigerator. At the back of the garage was a door that would lead into the rest of the house. "I did not realize the door would lock behind me," the old woman said. "I hardly ever come out to the garage." She smiled and shook her head. "I must be so stupid!" There was the hint of an accent in the old woman's voice—the emphasized *oo* when she said *stupid,* the way *garage* ended in a breathy *shh*—so slight that, at first, Maria wasn't sure if perhaps she'd imagined it. "I know the doors will be locked," the old woman said. "I always lock them. But who knows, maybe I just do not have big enough muscles."

The house was no different from the others on the block. One story, brick, built on a concrete foundation that rose about three feet above the ground. Maria could imagine the layout inside: hallway running the length of the garage with doorways creating a circuit between the living room and kitchen. Bedroom and bathroom tucked away at the back of the house. She wondered whether it would be more conspicuous to take a moment to help an old woman or to refuse to do so. At worst, she supposed, this might be an alibi.

Maria rattled the front doorknob while the old woman stood at the bottom of the stoop, holding onto the wrought iron banister. Satisfied that it was locked, they walked around back, the old woman taking careful steps, one hand braced against the side of the house, chattering on about how clumsy and careless she must be, and Maria walking slowly, trying not to get too far ahead. In the backyard, Maria held the screen door open with her foot and pushed uselessly against the heavier wooden door behind it.

"Yes," the old woman said, "I thought it would be locked. But you know what? Here is the good news: there is a window in the front. I think that will be open. And my husband has a ladder in the garage."

They headed back toward the front, Maria trotting ahead this time, testing each window as they passed. She reached the front yard and decided to try the door at the back of the garage while the old woman was still making her way along the side of the house. Finding the door locked, Maria stood alone in the garage for a moment, looking around for the ladder. Lengths of extension cord drooped from hooks on the wall. Cobwebbed squares of plywood leaned behind an ancient push mower. Everything looked too old to be of any value, but Maria's imagination flickered, thinking of those television shows about antique hunters that her foster parents watched: there were always old people living in squalor, not realizing they owned some small fortune that was just gathering dust in a closet. A hazy plan took shape in her mind and she imagined climbing through a window and pocketing some priceless object before unlocking the door and letting the old woman inside.

Two boxes were stacked, one atop the other, next to the door at the back of the garage. The flaps of the top box were unfolded. Maria peeked inside. Wool coat, tweed pants. Men's brown leather wingtip shoes.

"There," the old woman said, finally appearing in the driveway. She pointed to the back wall of the garage, where the ladder rested horizontally on the floor. "If you can carry that out this way," she said. Maria obeyed. "My husband will not be home until late," the old woman explained again. "Otherwise, I would not mind waiting. But he is not home until after dark. Imagine me standing out here all night! He teaches—a professor—at the university. Department of Theology. I would call and ask him to come home, you know, but the telephone is inside, of course."

Maria leaned the ladder against the house, just below the window.

"I need to thank you," the old woman said. "I would be stuck out here in the dark if you hadn't come along. I am not keeping you, I hope? Do you live nearby?"

"Not too far," Maria said, not wanting to share any specific details.

"We are neighbors," the old woman said. "Tell me, what is your name? So that I can say hello when I see you walking. I have seen you walking before. From my window, in the evenings. You come back and forth down this street. Back and forth, always. You are looking for something?"

Maria let the question go. She wiped cobwebs from the ladder onto the leg of her jeans. She decided to give a fake name, just in case. "My name is Melissa," she said. It was the first name that popped into her mind—a popular girl from school who ran track and ate salads for lunch.

"Melissa," the old woman repeated. "Such a pretty name. And I am Ania." They shook hands. "And now, we will say hello. My husband, Danek—he knew many more neighbors. Always out here, waving hello to people. But I am not so sociable and many of the neighbors we used to know do not live here anymore. That begins to happen when you get to be my age. I am seventy-eight years old!" Ania cried, her small voice rising in disbelief. "Oh, well. Now I know your name—Melissa!—and now I will wave and say hello when you pass, and the next thing you know, I will be showing up at your house for dinner!"

An involuntary sound escaped Maria's throat, something between a scoff and a giggle.

"Oh, I'm kidding, I'm kidding," Ania said. "Your parents, are they good cooks? Ha! I'm kidding. You should not listen to me.

I joke around too much. I am always joking around. I must drive people crazy! But you are a tall and strong girl. Your parents must feed you well."

Maria stepped up onto the ladder. She didn't want to talk about her parents. As far as she was concerned, she didn't even have parents. A mom she could hardly remember and a dad she'd never met. And the family she lived with now, The Lawrences. Who even were they? Two nice middle-class people who went to church every Sunday and who Maria didn't seem to share anything with beyond the dim enjoyment of the boxed macaroni and cheese that they brought home each week from the supermarket.

"Seventy-eight years old," Maria said, hoping to change the subject. "That means you were born in . . ."

"1933," Ania said. "My husband and I have lived in this house for over forty years now. 1960s, we came to the United States."

"I thought you had an accent," Maria said.

"From Poland. We lived first in New York. You know, that is where all the immigrants used to arrive. We came upstate for the university. For my husband." Maria was up on the ladder now, the old woman prattling on from the ground below. "I wish he would have retired a long time ago. If you think that I have thick glasses, you should see his! I joke that he can hardly see what he is writing on the blackboard anymore. Always he is walking around the house, looking for his watch or his wallet. He is constantly misplacing things. He gets so frustrated, but it is because he can hardly see what is right in front of him!"

Maria braced her feet against the sides of the ladder and pushed upward on the window as hard as she could. The seam between sill and frame widened only a tiny bit. She put her face to the glass and peered into the house. The other side of the window was bordered by thin, white curtains, and beyond her reflection, she could make out the dim contours of the darkened interior—an armchair, the corner of a coffee table. She looked upward along the inside of the window frame and let out a breath of disappointment when she noticed the small shape of the latch sticking out over the rail that divided the two panes; the window was locked.

"He will lose his glasses," Ania went on, "and I always ask him, 'well, where was the last place you saw them?' And, oh my gosh, you would not believe—he will begin to walk backwards through the entire house, retracing his steps. Can you imagine? An old man like that, half-blind, his hair uncombed, usually dressed in nothing but his underwear—a university professor!—and here he is, walking around backwards?"

Maria smiled, waiting for a gap in the old woman's chatter.

"Forty years, we've lived here," Ania went on, "and many years in New York before that. Manhattan. Bronx. But we did not like the city so much. Tiny little apartments. And the noise! It was France before that. And before that, Poland. You get to be so old and you can hardly believe all the different places you have seen. All the things you have lived through." She sighed. Maria began to speak but before she could get a word out, Ania held up her arm and said, "Here, let me show you something." And Maria watched from atop the ladder as the old woman pulled up the sleeve of her cardigan. Thin lines were tattooed beneath the pale skin of her forearm. The ink, faded, the same blue as her veins. "I was very small then," Ania said. "Seven years old when my family was taken to Germany." Only then did Maria recognize the tattoo as numbers. "My husband, Danek, he was older. Eleven years old when he was brought to Plaszow. A work camp."

Maria bit her lip, unsure of how to respond. "Jeez," she said. "Wow." The words sounded clumsy and childish. She wasn't sure what to say about something like this.

"It was easier for me, perhaps," Ania said, a sad half-smile dreaming its way along the corner of her mouth. "I was young. A child knows how to keep quiet and go unnoticed. A child knows how to pretend." Her gaze pointed somewhere down the street, where the block ended and the road disappeared into the park. The sky was still light, but the moon was visible, a dim hook fishing over the trees.

Maria cleared her throat. "I don't think I can get this open," she said. "It's locked."

Ania nodded. "Yes. I thought as much."

Maria stepped down from the ladder, and the ground, when the toe of her shoe touched, felt like it was floating, like it would drift off from beneath her.

"How long until your husband will be home?" Maria asked, but the old woman did not seem to hear.

"I tell you what we will do," Ania said. "You break the glass." She was already shuffling toward the garage. Maria watched Ania push things around on the tool bench until she found a hammer.

"Listen," Maria said, "I really should be getting home."

"Do not be worried," Ania said. "You just—*pow!*—and climb through. It takes no time at all. You are tall and strong. You will be good at this, I know it." Her voice had become stern, flat, filled with a worrying authority. Her heavy cheeks drew deep lines along either side of her mouth, and Maria could hear the old woman's breath moving in and out through her nostrils. "It does not matter," Ania said. "A broken window? We will pretend. Like children. We will say that it was something else—some boy threw a rock," she said, "or perhaps a burglar came in. Such things happen in this neighborhood." The old woman held the hammer out in front of her, a ball-peen, the handle flecked with white paint. The neighborhood was quiet. A dog's leash jingling on the other side of the street. The whir of a car accelerating the next block over. Maria took the hammer and looked back at the window.

"Okay, okay," Ania said. She looked down at the ground, pouting. "I must apologize. I have not been honest with you. You have given your whole evening to me, a stranger, and I repay you with dishonesty. But we know each other now. You are Melissa. You are Melissa and I am Ania and we are friends. We are neighbors. I do not want for you to walk past my house every evening and think that this is the home of a liar. Really, Melissa, I lie to myself. Because I am not used to this yet." A sound came from her throat that Maria thought might be the beginning of tears. "I am alone here," Ania said. "My husband, Danek—I tell you that he is coming. I tell myself that he is coming. But it is two weeks now. His heart," she said. Then she stood quietly, looking down at her feet. "They take him to the hospital and—" but the words caught in her throat, and all Ania could do was hold her hands out in front of her.

Maria thought of the boxes in the garage. Men's clothes. The hammer seemed to grow heavier in her grip. She tightened her fingers around the handle, then took Ania by the hand. The old woman's grip was frail, her fingers dry and warm. Maria led her back across the lawn. She stepped up onto the ladder again. The streetlights were glowing now, the last pink of sun cutting across the horizon and burning in the spaces between houses. She lifted the hammer and when she brought it down, she was surprised how easily the glass broke. In the jagged opening, she could see the living room clearly, its plain furniture, its clean, blank walls.

Curved triangles of glass clung in the window frame like teeth. She tapped them out, the shards landing silently on the carpeted floor inside. Ania's voice came from behind her. "Here," the old woman said. She was holding up the wool coat from the box of Danek's clothes. "Put this down so you do not cut yourself."

Maria draped the coat over the windowsill and leaned through the empty square. A breath of curtain moving against her forearm as she cantilevered over the broken glass, arms stretching and fingers carefully touching down on the soft grain of carpet. She had the feeling of climbing into the mouth of some great beast. She crouched on the floor, breathing in the air of the house. A clock ticking somewhere in the dark. The soft crunch of glass like dead leaves beneath her shoe. From inside, the square of night in the window seemed as distant as if she were staring up from the bottom of a well. Sitting in the dark, she felt, for a moment, utterly alone, until finally there was Ania's tiny voice from outside again: "On the hook, by the door. The keys."

Once inside, Ania turned on the lights, and Maria helped to vacuum the broken glass. When they were through cleaning, Ania offered a glass of water, but Maria insisted that she needed to be on her way.

"Melissa," Ania said, "you cannot leave without some thanks, my dear Melissa." Maria wished she hadn't given the fake name, wished she could undo the lie. She thought of how vulnerable the old woman had been, how helplessly she had allowed Maria to lead her across the lawn. Ania disappeared toward the back of the house, and the girl stood alone in the living room. A small upright piano took up one corner. A coffee table and a worn armchair. The plaster bust of a man's head on the end of a mantel that was lined with small ceramic figurines: a pig, a cow, a little boy wearing a straw hat. Books lined a shelf, heavy volumes with frayed, leathery spines. An end table with a doily and a framed photograph, black and white, of two little girls, each in flowered dresses not unlike the one Ania wore now.

"I won't eat them," Ania said. She had reappeared suddenly, pushing a box of gingersnaps toward the girl. "They will go to waste. Have as many as you want. Please, take them. As a thank you."

Maria took one cookie, chewed it slowly, almost fearfully.

"And something else," Ania said. "Do not move. I owe you more than just thanks. I owe an apology, as well." Ania shuffled off again and when she returned, she carried a small wooden jewelry box. She sat down in the armchair and set the box on the coffee table. "Do you wear rings?" Ania said. She was picking through delicate chains tangled among gaudy brooches, rings with wide opal stones, dangling earrings. "I never wear this junk anymore," she said. "Who would I be trying to impress? Let's find the most expensive one. I will not miss it. Look at me. Like some old dragon nesting on my jewels. Here, here, pick something. As a thank you. And to apologize for behaving so foolishly before. I promise, whatever you take, I will not miss it."

Maria stood across the room, growing more and more embarrassed by the old woman's gratitude. "I don't know," Maria said. "I need to be going. I don't really—"

"Nonsense. Come, take your reward. You have earned it. I have no use for these things."

Maria took a few steps forward, peered over the lid of the box. "Really, I don't need anything," she said, but Ania gave a dismissive wave.

"Here," the old woman said. "You sit down and pick something out. Take your time, Melissa. I don't need to hover over you like a vulture! I will go and make something to celebrate." The old woman's eyes went wide. "Some tea! Yes, I'll make us some tea." Then she turned and hobbled toward the kitchen.

"Really," Maria pleaded, following after her. There was the sound of pots and pans clanging as Ania rummaged through a cupboard.

"It will not take long! I have this wonderful box of herbal—"

"Please," Maria said. "I can't stay. My parents . . ." She paused. "My mom will be expecting me home."

Ania exhaled, nodding her head, collecting herself. "Of course, of course. You must be going. I'm so sorry." She smiled. "I've kept you long enough. Let me walk you to the door."

As they moved back through the living room, Ania stopped and bent over the jewelry box. She picked out a silver brooch shaped like a flower with a blue stone embedded in the center. "Here," Ania said. "I made a fast decision for you." She gave Maria a tiny smile. "It belonged to my sister." Maria waited while the old woman carefully pinned the brooch to her shirt. "Beautiful," Ania said.

"Thank you," Maria said.

"Thank you, thank you," the old woman repeated. "What is she thanking me for? I should be thanking her! This is what happens when you get to be my age. You begin to do everything backwards!" Ania laughed, then sighed. "Please," she said, "any time you are passing by, I want you to visit. Any time you are out walking, Melissa, back and forth, like you do. I will make sure the door is not locked again. Please. Let yourself in. My home is your home. We will be friends now."

The sky was dark by the time Maria left, and as soon as the door was closed behind her, she ran. Across the lawn, down the block, through the park. The silver brooch bouncing against her chest. She ran past the playground and basketball courts and the small pond where the sound of crickets and bullfrogs rose in a siren crescendo. She ran until she was back at the Lawrences', through the kitchen and upstairs, where, behind the closed door of her bedroom, beneath the warm blankets of her bed and the plastic stars fixed to her ceiling, she curled up and closed her eyes and listened to the slow sound of her own breath until, gradually, the world settled itself back into something almost familiar.

That night, the breeze that came through Ania's window was warm. Since her husband's death, she had not been able to sleep in her bed—the bed that they had shared for more than forty years. Instead, she sat in the armchair in the living room, facing the empty window frame, Danek's wool coat spread over her legs. As soon as the girl left, the house had felt empty, and Ania had immediately felt alone and ashamed. Pathetic, she thought. Forcing her company on some poor girl. She felt stupid for having told the girl about Danek and she felt stupid for having brandished the tattoo the way she had. Too much and too soon for some stranger who had no reason to concern herself with the loneliness and bad memories of a sad, old widow. Ania hadn't been able to help herself.

She told herself to remember, in the morning, to unlock the back door. Despite what she had told the girl, she hadn't always kept the doors locked. Only now that she was alone. But what do I have to be afraid of? she thought, and she sat awake for a long time, staring out at the night.

When she closed her eyes, the darkness behind her eyelids was, as it always was, a familiar one. It was the darkness of a crowded train car. The open mouth of a rifle. Sometimes, when she slept, she was a girl and she was in Lublin, standing in front of her mother in the creaking warmth of the apartment where she had taken violin lessons as a child, and she sometimes realized, in the middle of her lesson, that the song she was scratching her way through was one that she wouldn't have known until a few years later, a piece she heard played from a distance, every morning, by the prisoners' orchestra during the long hours of roll call. Always, she woke with sore feet, as if she had been standing all night in her dreams.

Wind rustled the trees outside. The house settled. Floorboards sighed and the radiator clicked. Ania drifted toward sleep and amid the sounds of the house, she was certain, for a moment, that she heard Danek's soft footsteps moving on the carpet behind her. She sat up, suddenly awake, and said her husband's name aloud to the dark. But it was nothing. Occasionally a car drove by, headlights illuminating the room and casting long shadows across the walls and ceiling, and though they were stretched out and distorted, Ania recognized their shapes: the bust on the mantel, the bookshelf with its sharp corner lunging across the wall, the doorknob of the closet from which she had packed up Danek's coat earlier that morning. Ever since she was young, Ania had always been afraid of the dark. But she remembered now the soft pull of Danek's arms around her whenever she couldn't sleep, whenever she woke from nightmares—nightmares that she never needed to explain to him. *What is the dark but a shadow,* he would say. *An outline left by the sun. The memory of something that is no longer there.* No shadow was out of place here now. There was the shadow of the piano, where Danek would sometimes tinker with simple melodies from his head. The coffee table, where he would spread the newspaper each morning and read aloud from the comic strips—a ritual that began in their tiny apartment in the Bronx, when she and Danek were first trying to learn English, and which continued on for years and years, even after their favorite strips had gone out of print. She remembered how, whenever Danek misplaced his glasses—he always left them in the same place, right there, on the edge of the mantel—she would sit in the armchair where she sat now and stare at them while he walked around the house, sometimes backward, half-blind, cursing, wondering aloud where he'd left them, until she could no longer hold in her laughter, and she would call out, warmer, Danek, or colder, Danek, or for Heaven's sake, you dummy, they are in the same exact place where you always leave them, there on the corner of the mantel, where they still sat, a small triangle of light caught in the thick glass and reflected onto the dark wall behind.

SHIT PLATE

For a whole week, Mike Cobb had been swinging around this gold chain necklace that he bought with money saved up from playing Shit Plate at lunch. Shit Plate was short for Mike Cobb's Million Dollar Shit Plate, which Kyle Scheuller always hollered out in this game-show-host voice, like, "Welcome, folks, to today's episode of *Mike Cobb's Million Dollar Shit Plate!*" It was a game where we all mixed up the grossest stuff from our school lunches, then put down whatever change was in our pockets, and if Mike ate the whole thing, he'd get to keep the money.

Kids at school always picked on Mike, called him Dirty Mike or Cobb the Slob. But he was a nice enough guy. He was quiet and always walked down the hall staring at his feet. He wore stained, oversized T-shirts, sometimes for two or three or four days in a row. I remember hearing that his mom was in jail, or that maybe she had gone crazy and was locked up in a mental hospital.

But after Mike bought that gold chain, he was a whole different person. Like the chain was some sort of badge of his worth.

Like he wasn't poor anymore since he'd been able to afford this one expensive thing. J. J. Minelli asked him why he didn't just put the stupid chain around his neck like he was supposed to. "It's called a necklace, dummy. *Neck*-lace. Quit swinging it around like a fucking jump rope." Mike just smiled, made a big fart noise with his mouth, and that was that.

Mike had been saving up since Christmas break, ever since they raised the price of school lunch—it went from just sixty-five cents to costing over a dollar. Before the holidays, the PTA sent home fliers explaining how the school board had voted to start serving healthier food, like fresh bananas and granola bars, and it would cost a little more but would be worth it to provide us kids with the nutrition that we need. But once that happened, Mike never had enough money for lunch—I don't know if his grandma couldn't afford it or what. To some of us who sat with Mike at lunch every day, Shit Plate felt like a good thing that we were doing, like charity. Mike never went hungry when he sat at our table, and sometimes he made as much as four or five dollars in a day.

The day that Mike bought the gold chain was the first and only time I ever went to his house. It was the last couple weeks of the school year and my own house was a mess of boxes. My dad had gotten a big promotion, and so my parents bought a new house out in Manlius. It was a lot bigger than the house we were living in, and Dad said that we might finally be able to get a trampoline in the backyard. After we moved, he said, I was going to be in a new school district. They were going to send me to a private school where I'd have to wear a uniform every day. I wasn't exactly thrilled, but the idea of private school somehow felt important, and my parents talked about it like it would be a really meaning-ful part of my life. "Ten years from now," my dad said, "when you have a good job, you'll be glad you did it." I hadn't told any of my friends about the move yet. But my mom was glad for any oppor-tunity to get me out of the house while she packed, so probably she was thankful when Mike called to ask if I wanted to stay over at his house on Friday night. Dad even slipped me twenty bucks that morning. "In case you guys want to order a pizza or something."

I wasn't in the habit of hanging out with Mike aside from at lunch, but I figured it wasn't a big deal if I hung out with him this one time since I'd be moving soon, anyway. And I guess I felt sort of bad for him. I don't know that Mike really had any friends outside of our lunch table.

Mike's house was practically the last stop on the school bus. We had to go through all these neighborhoods that I didn't even recognize. The streets were lined with dollar stores and auto repair garages where guys in gray jumpsuits sat in lawn chairs on the sidewalk. By the time we got to Mike's house, I was feeling hot and dizzy from bouncing around in the back seat of the bus for so long. There was a tall set of cracked cement steps leading up to his house, which sat on the side of a hill along a busy road. Even though it was sunny outside, the inside of Mike's house was dark. Sunlight baked through the cracks in the blinds and the whole house had a smell like the inside of a microwave.

Mike's room was empty except for a plain mattress on the floor and a huge pile of dirty clothes that spilled out of the closet. The first thing he did was dump a pocketful of change into this big coffee can that he had stashed up on a shelf in his closet. It was mostly full of coins, but there were dollar bills crumpled up in there too, and it was filled almost to the top. It was probably the most money I'd ever seen in my entire life. I remember, when he pulled the coffee can down, all the change shifting around made it sound like one of those African rain sticks that they've got in the music room at school—those long bamboo things that are filled with beans or rice or whatever, and when you tip them over, it sounds like rain. After he took the coffee can out of his closet and added the money from that day's shit plate, Mike took off his shirt and went digging through the clothes on his floor for a new one. Then he stuffed the coffee can into his backpack and asked if I wanted to go to the mall.

The mall was almost three miles away, so we rollerbladed, and the whole time Mike had that coffee can sloshing around in his backpack, which only had one strap on it. The other strap had been ripped sometime last year when these kids jumped him on the playground after school, and he'd been walking around with that torn strap dangling behind him like a tail ever since.

We rollerbladed along the divider on Erie Boulevard with cars shooting past in both directions and barely enough room for us to skate beside each other. Pebbles kept getting caught in my wheels, and I was afraid I was going to pitch forward into traffic. When we finally got to the mall, we skated around in the parking lot for a while and took turns doing jumps off the wheel-chair ramp. Eventually, I followed Mike into the jewelry store, which was one of the only places at the mall that was still in busi-ness—there was the jewelry store and the movie theater, a vac-uum repair shop, a T.J. Maxx, and KB Toys—but the lady behind the counter told us we couldn't have rollerblades on inside the store, so we took them off and I sat out by a dry, empty fountain to make sure nobody stole them while Mike went back in wear-ing just his droopy old socks to look at the necklaces beneath the glass display counter. I could see from outside the store that the lady who worked there was watching Mike, like she didn't want him in there, even without his rollerblades. Finally, he pointed to something under the glass and when he unzipped his back-pack and put that coffee can on the counter, the lady shook her head and told him, "Uh-uh. You cannot pay for it like this." I don't know what the big deal was. Money is money, as far as I'm concerned. But the way she was looking at him, it was like Mike could've been handing her a crispy new hundred-dollar bill, and she still would've told him no.

We sat outside the store for a while, wondering what to do and flipping the lady off whenever she had her back turned. I grabbed a quarter from Mike's coffee can, closed my eyes, and said, "I wish for that lady to not be such a prick," and then I flipped the quarter into the fountain. Mike punched me hard in the arm and then climbed down and got the quarter back.

"What do you want that necklace for?" I kept asking, but Mike just smiled and shrugged.

"I dunno," he said. "It's cool."

We skated around the food court and asked if anyone could trade bills for Mike's coins. I didn't tell him about the twenty I had in my pocket because there was no way I was going to let him stick me with eighty quarters. The teenager at the pretzel place let us give him twenty quarters for a five, but nobody wanted all of those nickels and dimes and pennies. Finally, the guy at the vacuum repair place told us there was a bank across the street, so we skated back across the boulevard and helped the old lady who worked there count all of the coins into rolls. She traded Mike some bills and when we were done, Mike had $103.18.

A different lady was working at the jewelry store when we

got back and she was a lot nicer—she let us both leave our roller-blades by the register and walk around in our socks—but she still gave us a look: smiling, but furrowing her brow, like she didn't want us to know that she liked us.

Mike pointed at this necklace made up of tiny links that fit together like fish scales. It had a nameplate on it that spelled out *Brooklyn* in big cursive letters. The woman brought the necklace over to the register and Mike handed her all of his money, which didn't look like very much after it had been changed into bills.

"Where'd a kid like you get this much money?" the lady wanted to know.

"Mowing lawns," Mike lied.

"That's an awful lot of work for a kid your age. Must be for someone special. I bet it's a gift for your mom, huh?"

"Sure," Mike lied again.

"I wish my kids were this thoughtful," she said, and then she gift wrapped the necklace for no extra charge.

It was dark by the time we got back to Mike's house. His grandma still wasn't home from work, and so we put on MTV, turned off all of the lights, and danced to all of the rap videos from Nelly and Juvenile and Ruff Ryders. The whole time, Mike was wearing his new chain, holding it out in front of him with one hand while he raised the roof with his other. It was around nine o'clock when his grandma finally got home. As soon as he heard the front door, Mike ran to his room, took off his necklace, and hid it under his mattress. His grandma warmed up frozen fish sticks from a box and the three of us sat at the kitchen table and dipped them in ketchup.

"So, what grade are you in?" Mike's grandma said. She was looking down at her plate, and it took me a moment to realize she was speaking to me. I nodded toward Mike and said, "Sixth. We're both in the same grade."

"Well, I guess you two will be going into high school together pretty soon," she said, and I told her, "I guess so," even though high school was still two whole years away. Plus, I hadn't told Mike about how I'd be going to private school next year. "The two of you will be best friends if you're in high school together," she said, but she sounded sad, like she didn't quite believe what she was saying.

"You weren't scheduled to work tonight," Mike said to his grandma.

"No," his grandma said. "No, I wasn't." A fly buzzed over the table and landed in the ketchup on the side of my plate. Mike stared at his grandma and after a long silence, she sighed. "If you're asking me where I was, your uncle and me drove out to see your mom today."

She started saying something else, but Mike cut her off. "Why didn't you bring me?"

"Mike, hon," she said, "I told you a hundred times, it's not good for you to see her out there."

"Fuck you," Mike said, and it was so abrupt that, at first, I wasn't sure if he was really angry or if it was maybe like a joke where they pretended to be mad at each other.

"Mike," his grandma said.

They were both silent for a moment. I could see Mike's nostrils flair, his fist tighten around the fork in his hand. Then he clenched his teeth and said, "Bitch."

Mike's grandma sighed again, then stood up and put her plate in the sink. "There's pop-tarts in the cupboard for dessert," she said. She went upstairs and we didn't see her again for the rest of the night.

When it was late, Mike pulled the cushions off the couch and made a bed for me on the floor. He lay down on the bare couch frame and we watched TV in the dark until I heard him snoring. I muted the TV and listened to the sounds of cars driving by in the night until, after a long time, I fell asleep too.

About a week later, Mike and I were walking around after school and he was swinging the gold chain around as if it hadn't cost him half a school year of eating shit plates. We'd bought a bag of sunflower seeds at the gas station and were spitting the shells at different targets—mailboxes and stop signs and stuff like that. It was the last week of school and I was trying to get up the courage to tell him about how I was moving. I felt like I should say something, even if I still didn't really think of Mike as my friend.

"Here, bite it," Mike said, holding out the *Brooklyn* nameplate. I bit down on it. "See?" he said. "That's how you can tell it's real." I nodded, but I didn't know what biting the thing was supposed to tell me. I wondered why he had bought a chain that said *Brooklyn* when we lived in Syracuse. Then I wondered why none of the necklaces at the jewelry store even said *Syracuse.*

Mike was holding the chain up in front of him when a car stopped a little way ahead of us and a woman hopped out of the passenger side door.

"Mikey?" she hollered. "Mikey?" She had black hair that was so thin, even from far away, you could see her pale scalp showing through underneath. "Mikey, come here, baby," she said, and without a second's hesitation, Mike ran toward her, the chain swinging at his side. His backpack slipped off his shoulder and he didn't even stop to pick it up. I grabbed it and by the time I caught up to him, he and the woman were both standing in the road, and she was bending down, hugging him and kissing him all over his face, and Mike was smiling but also sort of squirming to get away. The skin around the woman's mouth was all pink and irritated, like maybe she'd been burned. I stood on the sidewalk, holding Mike's backpack.

"Hi, sweetie," she said when she noticed me standing there. She sort of whistled when she said the word *sweetie.* The car she'd hopped out of was just stopped in the middle of the road, engine still running, passenger-side door still hanging open. I couldn't see whether or not anyone was sitting in the driver's seat. She kissed Mike again and told him how happy she was to see him. "You getting good grades?" she asked, and Mike furrowed his brow and looked down at his feet. "Hey," she said. She crouched down in front of him. "Look at me when your mother asks you something. Are you getting good grades? Don't tell me you're flunking."

"What are you doing here?" Mike asked, and his mother made this exaggerated frown, like when a clown is pretending to be sad. Mike just stared at her, waiting. She stood up and went digging through her coat pockets until she found a pack of cigarettes. "Mom," Mike insisted, but she stood there flicking her lighter and not answering him until her cigarette was lit.

"Grandma taking good care of you?" she asked. "She giving you enough food?"

"Yeah," Mike mumbled.

"Yeah," his mom imitated. "Yeah. Yeah. Yeah." She cocked her head back and forth and made a little song out of it. "Yeah, yeah, yeah, yeah, yeah." Then she laughed really loud. She hugged Mike again. I'd never seen anyone do so much hugging before. "Baby, I'm so glad to see you," she said. She smiled and let out a puff of smoke, then nodded toward the gold chain that was still dangling from Mike's fist. "What's that?"

Mike started to say something, but his mom was already lifting his hand, his fingers already opening up like a clam revealing its pearl. She took the necklace and held it up in front of her face.

"Mikey, this is real gold?" she asked. "Oh, hun, this is really yours? Someone gave you this?" She stared at Mike for a long moment and then her face twisted up, suddenly disgusted, as if the necklace was a tangle of hair she'd just pinched from the drain. "Aw, no, you stole this, didn't you?"

"No, Mom," Mike begged. His voice was high and whiny like a little kid.

"Where'd you steal this from?"

Mike just stood there looking at the ground. I thought about speaking up, saying something about how hard-earned Mike's money was, how long he had been saving. But I couldn't stand to have his mother's attention on me.

"All right," she said. "All right. All right. That's okay. I understand. I'm not gonna pretend I'm perfect. Nobody's perfect. Especially not me. I know damn well that *I'm* not perfect. Listen," she said, and I could see little gobs of spit congealing at the corners of her mouth. "Listen to me. I'm gonna do you a favor, okay? I'm gonna hold onto this for you and keep it secret so that grandma doesn't catch you with it, okay? Grandma doesn't tolerate stealing. She sees this, she'll march you right back to wherever you took it from and make you embarrass yourself over the whole thing. And I ain't gonna let her do that." Her voice swelled to a proud bravado. "Nuh-uh. Uh-uh. I'm your only mother," she said. "You came from out of me. I made you and nobody else is gonna be allowed to embarrass you except for me." She laughed, and then she glanced at me and winked, like I was supposed to be in on some joke with her. "Listen," she said, turning back to Mike. "Listen to me. Listen." She pointed a finger close to Mike's nose. With her arm extended, the sleeve of her shirt rode up a little bit and I could see that there were dark bruises around the knobs of her wrist. "You're a good kid," she said. "You are a sweet, sweet baby," and she reached down and pinched his cheek. "I don't want you flunking. And I don't want you stealing. You're a good boy and I don't fuckin' want this shit." She held the necklace right up in front of Mike's face. "You hear me? I don't want this shit."

"I didn't steal it," Mike said.

"I gotta tell you something," his mom said. "Okay?"

Mike didn't respond.

"Okay?" she practically yelled, and Mike nodded. "They're probably telling you that I'm in that hospital again, right? That's what grandma is telling you?" She stood up straight, smiled, shook her head. She looked up at the sky for a moment and muttered some stuff that didn't sound like words, then scoffed and laughed and then scoffed again. "That's lies," she said. "That's lies. You got that? I'm here, aren't I? This is where I am. I'm right here. Right?"

"Okay," Mike said.

"Can't be in two places at once, can I? I'm right here. Don't forget that. Now come here," she said. "Gimme a hug." The gold chain dangled from her fist as she hugged him. Mike seemed to wither in her arms. "You're a good kid," she said. "I'm gonna come get you soon. Okay? I'm gonna come get you and we'll live together again. Okay?" She kissed him on the cheek with her weird, burned mouth, then turned around and hopped in the car. The brake lights glowed red for a second and then the car sped off and I stood there holding Mike's backpack and he stood there holding nothing.

The next day, J. J. and Kyle mixed up a shit plate of mayonnaise and apple sauce and red Jell-O with bananas. The money on the table was just change—fifty-three cents, which wasn't even enough for Mike to be able to buy a school lunch.

Thinking back on it, I wish I had just let Mike say, *No way. Not enough.* I wish I had let him push the shit plate back across the table. I wish I had let him go hungry. But I was thinking about how I hadn't spoken up to his mom. I felt so sorry for Mike, and watching everybody pull out their empty pockets, I got this impulse. I reached into my wallet and put down the twenty-dollar bill that my dad had given to me that day Mike and I went to the mall.

"Are you freaking crazy?" J. J. Minelli screamed. He stood up so fast that his chair fell over. "Twenty big ones—are you freaking crazy?" Everyone began cheering and laughing and drumming on the edges of the table.

"Welcome, folks," Kyle Scheuller crooned, "to today's very, very, very special episode . . ."

But before he even finished, Mike had lifted a dripping sporkful and shoved it into his mouth. Then another. And another. His spork clawed against the styrofoam tray. I wished for J. J. or Kyle to snatch the twenty and run. I wished that one of the lacrosse bullies like Spencer Pearson or James Archacki would come over and yank Mike's chair out from under him. I wished for some disruption that would send us all scattering across the cafeteria like roaches. Anything to get Mike to stop eating. He chewed slow, his mouth opened so that all of us could see each bite squish between his teeth and get pushed around by his tongue. The bell rang and Mike sat there, scraping up the last few bites, running his tongue along the front of his teeth. When the shit plate was clean, he pocketed the twenty and hustled off without saying anything.

By then, it was mid-June and there were just a couple days left in the school year. I don't know if Mike was absent those days or if he finally decided to sit at a different table. I went straight home after school and Mom gave me some boxes to start packing all the stuff in my room. My baseball cards and video games and CD player. After I packed up most of my stuff, I helped my mom clear out the attic. Winter coats and extra blankets and the tent that we'd bought for camping last summer. Other things—like my sister's old car seat and the cheap set of wine glasses that my mom had gotten in some free giveaway, pieces of old Halloween costumes and the crutches from when I broke my leg in second grade—we drove that stuff to the Salvation Army store and donated it. There was a lot of old stuff like that—things we didn't need, things we didn't want to take with us.

THE WRONG HOUSE

They had come to the wrong house, by which I mean they had come to our house. I answered the door and saw the two men in uniforms—paramedics laden with red canvas medical bags, each with a hand on the stretcher they had guided up our bumpy driveway. Behind me, the kids were racing up and down the stairs and screaming—some game in which they pretended to be caught in an avalanche—and I had to ask the man at the head of the stretcher to repeat himself.

"You've got the wrong address," I told him. "There's no emergency here." He repeated the address once more, and I pointed at the dark road behind them. The sun was setting and the sky looked like bruised flesh. Like a housefire. "That should be another block or two down, I think."

He muttered into the radio that was clipped to his epaulet. Then he apologized and I watched them drag the stretcher back to their truck. In another moment, there was the rumble of diesel. I closed the door and watched the flashing lights disappear down the road.

"What was that about?" my wife wanted to know.

"Wrong house," I told her.

"Can they do that?"

"Everyone makes mistakes."

I sulked back to the couch, took out my phone. The kids were shouting, "Help, help! We're trapped!" I scrolled past news clips about the war, footage of bodies buried under rubble. I was just looking for the score of the Pirates' game.

"What do you think it was?" my wife asked. "The emergency, I mean." She had moved to the window, was pulling the curtain and looking out in the direction the ambulance had driven. I was tired from work. From the kids screaming. I didn't feel like talking.

"Who knows," I said.

"I hope it wasn't anything serious. Like a stabbing or a shooting or anything."

I kept scrolling on my phone. The Pirates were up by three.

"Well, what do you think it was?"

I shrugged and closed my eyes and tried not to listen to the sound of the kids' feet clomping up and down the stairs—up and down, up and down. I turned on the television, found the game. Bottom of the sixth.

"Well," she said, "I sure hope the ambulance gets there in time."

There was the thump-thump-thump of the kids sledding down the staircase on a pillow. I shouted at them to knock it off.

"They've been at that game all day," my wife said.

"Why haven't you made them stop?"

"Would you rather they stare at a screen instead?"

I sighed, turned up the volume. I imagined drifting out of my body like some cartoon character's soul, floating over the city and landing behind third base with a hot dog and a beer.

"It's kind of eerie, isn't it?" my wife said. She was looking out the window again. "That they would come to the wrong house. Like there's a parallel universe where *we* have had some sort of accident. Like they crossed over from another timeline or something." She sighed in a way that sounded like longing. Why anyone would long for an accident was beyond me. "I wonder if they'll mention it on the news," she said. "I mean, if it is something serious."

"Listen," I said, "if you want my opinion, it's probably just some old lady who fell down or forgot to take her medication. It's probably some fucking geezer who's a breath away from death anyway. Can I watch this inning now, please?"

She turned away from me and looked out the window again. I had snapped at her—not because I'd wanted to, only because I was tired. I was hungry. I didn't make enough money. The kids clomping up and down the steps were driving me nuts and my life hadn't turned out quite like I'd imagined. I sighed and turned off the television and began to summon an apology. The children ran up the stairs again and in the moment of quiet when they reached the top, I could hear the sound of a siren outside. I looked to the window and in the black night, I could see the red and blue lights strobe past—hurrying back, I supposed, in the direction of the hospital. The lights disappeared and the window was black again and in that black was the sad reflection of my wife's face as she stared out into the endless night. There was the thunder of feet on the staircase, then a loud thud. One of the kids began to scream.

THE CURSED TREASURE OF
THE McDANIELS KIDS

Mom couldn't understand why we were so interested in him, the old man who shuffled through the park, waving his metal detector over the thick summer grass, digging up hubcaps and toothbrushes and bolts clodded with rust-colored dirt, bent nails, flattened sardine tins, and old roof tiles that came apart in his hands like fish scales. We couldn't explain it either. We only knew that we were fascinated by him. With his wispy hair and loose suspenders and face crowded between bulky, square-shaped headphones, his thick, round, wire glasses sliding down his nose toward an avalanche of gray-blonde mustache, the cord of the metal detector wrapped tight between his liver-spotted fingers, he was like something from another world, like something out of one of the old black and white science-fiction movies that sometimes played on Sunday mornings.

We never knew his name, but Mom said he was a retired cop, that he used to teach the anti-drug program at Edward Smith Elementary when she was a kid. "We called him Officer Friendly," she said, "but now, I don't know, he's just a bored old man with a hobby. I don't get why you kids follow him around the way you do."

My sister Angie—it was her idea to start burying things for him. "Like how pirates bury treasure," she said. Angie had a beat up lockbox from the flea market with a busted lock so that the lid flipped open if you tipped it. We filled it with clay sculptures we'd made at art camp—a pinch pot bowl and a couple little animals with broken legs and horns—and fake gold coins from an old Halloween pirate costume, and then we chose a spot and buried the box with a note: *HERE LIES THE CURSED TREASURE OF THE McDANIELS KIDS.*

We hid up in the maple tree and watched him dig up the box, slowly approaching the hump of dirt where it was buried, the search coil hovering over the grass, brushing left and right before settling on the exact spot, and then the old man unfolding the collapsible shovel at his belt and working it down through the dry earth. He crouched and opened the box and weighed the objects in his hands. He peered over his shoulder, suspicious, then stood, tucked the box under his arm, kicked the dirt back over the hole, and shuffled home.

After that, we gathered as much junk as we could find. Enamel pins and bottle caps and magnetic pieces from a board game we had outgrown, pennies and paper clips, a toy sheriff's badge that said *LONE STAR* on the front. We spilled mom's junk drawer and took keys we'd lost the locks for, belt buckles and dead batteries and a handful of old keychains from the Erie Canal Museum gift shop. From the attic, we gathered mangy Christmas tinsel and an ugly set of rectangular aluminum plates imprinted with designs of birds and flowers that Great Aunt Ruthy had given us years before. We gathered things that weren't even metal—pieces of broken action figures and plaster fossil replicas—and buried them along with whatever cans we could dig out of the recycling bin. We wrapped all of it in handkerchiefs or newspaper or plastic shopping bags and we buried it with notes that said things like *BEWARE!* or *DO NOT OPEN UNTIL X-MAS.* Angie soaked the notes in tea or singed them over the stove to give the appearance of ancient scrolls.

Sometimes the old man would appear half-dressed, wearing a bathrobe and slippers, a yellowed tank top, and baggy flannel pajama pants. We watched him from the tree line as he combed the field, going over the same spots again and again, like he'd forgotten what he was doing, or like he had dropped his keys and was looking around where he knew they should be. Sometimes he was out there all day, a silhouette in the dark before he finally made his way back across the street at the far end of the field to the little gray ranch house where he lived. There were moments when he would suddenly stop and look around—at the pond where families with strollers threw bread to ducks, or at the woods where we hid, watching from the branches of the old maple tree—and then he'd stare down at the machine in his hands as if he'd suddenly woken from a dream. But each time the metal detector caught a signal, the old man would come to life, would begin walking more quickly, leaning forward almost horizontally, as if he could sniff out our treasure from beneath that mustache, as if he could see with x-ray vision straight down through the earth. We noticed, after some time, that he'd begun carrying a flip pad in his shirt pocket, would jot notes before filling the holes back in and walking home with whatever we'd buried.

One day, we came home to find Mom sitting in the kitchen and crying. "The tuning fork," she sobbed. "Your dad's tuning fork." We could barely remember the object let alone Dad ever having used it. Maybe once or twice with the church choir when we were babies. But it was one of the few things of his that Mom had held onto. Angie looked at me with panic in her eyes and I immediately knew what had happened.

Without talking about it, we decided that we had to get the tuning fork back, and the next afternoon, we hid in our usual spot in the maple tree, Angie restlessly plucking leaves and tearing at them until she held only the skeletons of veins. It seemed forever before the old man arrived, and when he did, the wind blew his wispy hair around and made it stick up in a bizarre horn.

"What should we say to him?" I asked Angie. She made no response. I knew she meant to sit in the tree until the old man was headed back home. We watched him amble through the field, following the signal through his headphones until, like a dog with a scent, he paused and walked in a quick little circle toward the exact spot. He exhumed the treasure, and we saw that it was a coffee can we'd filled with severed doll parts. He tucked it under his arm and when he turned to leave, we shimmied down from the maple tree, following him at a distance and lingering behind when he reached the end of the field. I kept nudging Angie, telling her, "Go ask him, go ask him," and she hissed back, "I will, I will, shut up, I will." She was two years older than me and most certainly had been the one to bury the tuning fork in the first place, so we both knew that any dirty work was going to be up to her.

At the end of the field, the old man waited for traffic, then scuttled across the road toward his little gray ranch house. The screen door clapped behind him. A massive satellite dish perched on the roof, the sun setting pink above. We stood at the end of his driveway, churning gravel beneath the toes of our shoes, wondering how we would possibly explain ourselves. When it seemed there was nothing else to do, Angie pinched herself as hard as she could, then marched up to the door. She stood on the stoop, getting up the nerve to knock.

A garage was attached to the side of the house, and from the driveway, I could see movement through the windows of the roll-up door. I crept up and put my face to the glass.

"Angie," I whispered, but she didn't hear.

Inside the garage, a yellow light illuminated a rough wooden table cluttered with junk. The old man was picking doll parts from our coffee can and carefully placing them alongside what I realized were all of our things, everything we'd buried—the belt buckles and jewelry and coins and toys, the keychains and Christmas ornaments and everything. I knew that somewhere on the table was the tuning fork. I whispered for Angie again, my breath fogging the dirty glass. Beside each item, I could see, was a folded paper tent with a number—evidence markers, like you see in cop movies. On the wall, a corkboard with notes and newspaper clippings and lengths of thread stretching toward pins that were stuck into a crinkled map. Our whole lives on that table, spread out like a museum or an altar or a crime scene. I turned again to Angie—her fist raised to knock—and I cried out in horror of whatever mystery the old man thought he'd dug up.

YOU HAVE TO TALK
TO MARY ANNE

For Bill Lychack

You can't walk up 46th Street without talking to Mary Anne. She's always there, sitting in the lawn chair on her porch in her pink or gray sweatpants, and she's always talking—to the neighbors, to the mailman, to the landlord who's renovating two houses down, the dads pushing baby strollers, the women out jogging. "Where ya going?" she wants to know. "Where ya headed?" She sits there with a flyswatter in her hand, calling out to whoever passes by. She doesn't swat flies as often as she swats herself. Any time she cracks a joke, her lips pull back around her toothless gums and she raises the fly swatter, brings it down on her knee. "You're looking nice today," she says. "Are you picking me up for a date?" Swat. "They're saying the temperature tomorrow will be up in the eighties. Maybe I'll go put on my bikini!" Swat.

Mary Anne is eighty-one years old. She's lived in the same house since back in the '50s and has seen the neighborhood change in a million different ways. She remembers when the steel mills were still running and you could see the barges crawling slow along the Allegheny. She remembers when Saint Dominic's across the street was still open and all the old folks from the neighborhood used to fill the pews for Sunday mass. She remembers before the neighborhood started gentrifying, before they built those expensive townhouses on the next block up, before the young couples started moving in on either side of her. She doesn't mind. "Those are nice houses!" she tells you. She remembers all of this as she sits there in her lawn chair, calling out, "Where ya going? Where ya headed? Whatcha making for dinner later?"

You always stop for Mary Anne, whether you want to or not. She calls out to you while you're rushing down the sidewalk, on your way to work, already running late and trying to make it to the bus stop. "Where ya going?" she asks. She calls out when you're coming home tired with bags of groceries overflowing in both arms. "Whatcha making for dinner tonight?" Mary Anne loves to talk about whatever you're making for dinner tonight. "Me, I'm just making a boiled egg," she says. "I'm too tired." She complains about her son, Tommy, who is forty-six and still lives with her. "He can't cook," she says. "Forty-six years old and all he makes is spaghetti with meatballs. Can you believe he wants spaghetti with meatballs again tonight?" She leans over the railing like she's ready to tell you a secret. "That son of a bitch," she says, and she smiles, laughs, rocks back, brings the flyswatter down on her knee. "Spaghetti with meatballs, spaghetti with meatballs," she sighs. "I'm so dang sick of his spaghetti with meatballs."

Tommy works part-time for the diocese. Saint Dominic's has been boarded up for years, but the diocese still owns the building, and on weekends, you can see Tommy over there, running the Weedwacker along the side of the old church or stuffing garbage bags full of dead leaves. He's a broad-faced man with thin hair, always dressed in gym shorts and a sleeveless tee. Sometimes he's out there on the porch with Mary Anne, sitting below her on the concrete stoop, his legs splayed across the sidewalk, a case of IC Light resting under his arm and a cool can sweating in his grip. They'll sit out there in the long summer evenings, and you can hear the noise of the Pirates game from the television inside their house as you pass. Sometimes, Tommy runs an extension cord through a hole in the screen door so he can bring the radio out and listen to the game that way. When he's not at home, Tommy is usually sitting around in the dim light of Pollock's bar up on Liberty Avenue. Mary Anne tells you she saw on the news that somebody got stabbed in that place. "I always tell him," she says, "I always tell him, you don't need to be spending so much time up there. Some nasty place like that. I don't know why he hangs out there all the time." And then she leans forward, letting you in on another secret. "He's drinking is why. His father was the same way. I always tell him, what do you do that for? He don't need nothing like that. His father was the same way. And look where that got him. Died from his liver. Tommy don't need that."

Even in the rain, Mary Anne is sitting there in her lawn chair, the drops pounding down like machine gun fire on the aluminum awning above her porch, Tommy on the stoop below, legs stretched out to the sidewalk so that his sneakers get all wet. He doesn't seem to mind, and when you come hurrying down the sidewalk without your umbrella, trying to make it home before the storm picks up, he chuckles and shouts, "Looking a little damp there, buddy!" And before you pass, even in this weather, Mary Anne still leans forward from her seat and calls out to you. "I hear it's gonna be real bad tonight! Thunder and lightning!" You push the rain-slicked hair from your eyes and slow your pace for just a second, just out of politeness, trying to hear what she's saying over the noise of the rain, and that's all it takes—just like that, you're trapped, standing there trying to take shelter under the aluminum awning while she complains about the meteorologist on WPXI and asks again what you're making for dinner later. Eventually, Tommy shakes his head and says, "All right, Ma, he's getting soaked," and she tells you, "Hey, you better get home before the real storm comes," as if that isn't what you were trying for all along.

It gets so that a little prayer runs through your head whenever you walk up 46th. You look up at the granite angel in front of Saint Dominic's and even though you've never been religious, you offer your hopes up to whatever higher power there may be—a quiet plea that she'll have ducked inside for a moment, that she won't catch you, that you can just walk on by without having to stop and chat. Whenever you have to be somewhere, you leave the house a few minutes early, knowing that you'll be waylaid at Mary Anne's porch. You try walking on the other side of the street, but then you feel bad. You know she means well. And you don't want her gossiping with the others who walk by—you *know* she gossips. You don't want the other neighbors thinking that you're rude or stuck-up. And besides, even when you do walk on the other side of the street, she still calls out, still beckons you over. "Where ya going? Whatcha making for dinner later?"

She calls you over and asks your opinion of the decorations that she puts up in her front window. Paper chain of shining four-leafed clovers from the dollar store hanging over a slender vase filled with plastic white lilies. "I do it up special for Saint Patrick's Day," she says. "I do it up special, every year." A couple weeks later, she wants your opinion again. "I do it up special for Easter," she says. Prayer candles and ceramic angels arranged around the same plastic lilies. At the end of June, she bangs on the window from inside and waves to you while she's replacing the lilies with American flags for Independence Day. Mary Anne doesn't decorate for Halloween, though. She sees you coming home with bags of candy from Rite Aid and calls you over to tell you what she saw on the news. "Some guy was putting razor blades in candy and giving it out to little kids," she says, her eyes wide with disbelief. "They had it on the news. I couldn't believe it." You tell her that's just an urban legend, that they say the same thing every year, but Mary Anne shakes her head and wags her finger. "You got to watch out these days," she says. "You got to be very, very careful. Me, I'm just leaving my lights turned off this year. They don't celebrate Halloween like when I was a kid. You got to be very careful, I tell ya."

In November, when the temperature drops, Mary Anne isn't out on her porch anymore, but she still catches you, pokes her tiny head through the curtains and bangs on the window as you pass, as if she can sense your presence out there on the sidewalk. The vase where she sticks the lilies and American flags is replaced by a wicker basket full of dried gourds, and then by flickering electric candles and a ceramic nativity scene. By January, a crust of snow has gathered in the empty seat of her lawn chair, and walking to the bus stop in the cold, frozen mornings, you rub your hands together and feel thankful that you don't have to stop and talk. The streets are empty and sometimes you see Tommy salting the sidewalk along Saint Dominic's, a hard frown creasing his face. You can't help but wonder. Eighty-one years old. You know Mary Anne won't be around forever. You imagine Tommy standing in the dim light of a funeral parlor, sipping an IC Light, a baggy suit hanging on his body with the same fit as those gym shorts. On the weekend, you go out to dinner with friends, and passing Pollock's on your way home, Tommy stumbles out from inside, his face flushed, breath pouring out in thick plumes. The laces of his boots drag in the snow. You keep your eyes on the ground, sure that he doesn't recognize you. His head swivels around and he moans something drunk and unintelligible. Maybe it's your imagination getting the best of you, but when you think back on it later, you're sure the word was *Mom*. When you're a little further down the sidewalk, you hear a commotion, glance over your shoulder and see a couple other guys helping Tommy to his feet, brushing the snow off the arms of his coat.

Valentine's Day comes and goes with no sign of the plush cupid that Mary Anne hung from the window last year. The cold months pass, snow melting and running in steady currents along the curb down 46th. You trudge your way to the bus stop each morning, side-eying her window where the ceramic wise men and miniature farm animals still stand watch over baby Jesus. In April, Tommy is frowning, standing next to the church and jerking uselessly on the rip cord of his Weedwacker. It's not until the end of May when you're coming home in the evening from a long day of work, worn out and brain-dead, sweating through the back of your shirt, stomach rumbling, grocery bags splitting at their corners, when she suddenly hollers, "Hey, where the hell have ya been? I haven't seen you walking by lately," and you look up, smile, show her the kielbasa and salad fixings, happy to starve yourself for just a few moments longer.

LAKE SHORE LIMITED

A train pulls through the gray winter on the morning after Christmas. Sky still dark, snow melting in the drizzle of rain, windows fogged so the scenery ticking past feels almost like a secret—a peeling billboard, chewed-up utility pole, scrawl of graffiti—all of it glimpsed for just a breath before it's gone, miles behind, windows fogged again. Boston to Rensselaer, Rensselaer to Syracuse. That is the itinerary. But early in the trip, somewhere just outside Worcester, Massachusetts, a man leaps in front of the train and is killed.

At first, none of us know what has happened. The train slows to a rest. Two of us lean against each other in the seats, trying to will ourselves back to sleep. We search out each other's hands beneath the blanket of our coats, squeeze each other's fingers. Too early in the morning for conversation, but we likely wouldn't have much to say to each other anyway, exhausted from the ritual of holiday, the obligations of family, the days spent traveling, and exhausted to some degree, I can say now, with each other, the relationship funneling toward its end, even if we haven't yet realized it, even if we still whisper promises to each other in the night, voices hoarse with tears, clinging to one another like a child to a dream in the moments upon waking. I wish I could remember what any of the trouble between us was beyond the fact that we were young—nineteen, twenty-two—and when you feel like you need someone as desperately as we needed each other, you can't help but hurt the other person, can't help but be hurt, again and again and again. It was the kind of love where we punched walls because of how much we cared for each other. The kind of love where we pressed the tips of knives into our palms when the other person wasn't around.

We slip in and out of consciousness, dreams full of the sound of other passengers—coats shifting against seats, someone rooting through the overhead—and we hope that we will wake into some new life, some new version of ourselves, where we are happier and kinder, and where we don't feel lonely sitting next to one another.

Instead, we wake to the same gray view, rub the sleeves of our coats against the window to reveal the smokestacks bleeding into sagging rainclouds, the ends of railroad ties giving way to a ravine messy with gravel and slush, crumbling brickyards, slanted houses that must shake whenever the train rolls by, and everything dripping with rain, the horizon cropped with chain-link fence.

"How long have we been like this?" The first words either of us speak that morning, and it takes a moment for me to realize that you are talking about the train. I check my phone; nearly two hours since the train stopped. Passengers are standing now, chatting across the aisle, children watching cartoons on a laptop, the bright colors visible between the seats. A couple behind us talking about how there must be something wrong with the train, something mechanical that is being fixed, though by now, I can feel it—a grim knowledge taking shape in our minds, filling up the car. We all know something more is wrong than just the train and our imaginations can't help but darken. A mother quiets her toddler. Someone whispers, "It must be so horrible." The conductor walks hurriedly down the aisle toward the front of the train, fingers twisting the knob on his walkie-talkie so that, for a moment, the entire car is cut through with static.

When we've been stopped for nearly three hours, the conductor appears again, standing at the front of the car, announcing that, because of "police activity" on the track, the train cannot move forward. In another thirty minutes, we're all stepping out into the cold, lined up alongside the track, the porter directing us toward the back of the train, everyone hoisting luggage across the gravel ravine, then out onto the road, where a fleet of buses awaits. The clack of railroad replaced with the rumble of diesel, and on through the narrow streets, past darkened houses with strings of dead lights, the neighborhood filled with a gray hush, then a slow turn toward the on-ramp and the gentle rush of speed against the windows, hum of the road beneath us, your hand in mine again, huddled beneath our coats again, everyone still whispering, solemn and worrying and thankful to finally be on our way. And you and I wishing, silently, that there was anything—anything at all—that we could do to save ourselves.

All told, nothing else happened that day. The bus left us outside Albany, where we boarded another train north to Schenectady, then west, the sky dark again by that time, train barreling through the night, and on to Syracuse, a friend meeting us at the station, the two of us offering our yawns and tired laughter and thank-yous when we finally pull up in front of our little apartment on Clarendon Avenue. We sleep like rocks and in the morning, we scan the local news from Worcester until we find the headline: *Man Dies after Jumping in Front of Train.* I'll read the man's name, but by afternoon, I'll forget. Later, unpacking, I'll find the ticket stubs from our trip and I'll tuck them into a shoe box in the closet, thinking they're important but unable to tell myself why. It's not about me or you. And it's not about the dead man on the tracks. I'll remember looking through the fogged glass, you snoring gently, my jacket bunched between our shoulders. I'll lie awake at night, alone, years later, in a city hundreds of miles away from all that, and I'll hear the sound of a train whistle in the distance, and I'll think it is the most comforting sound in the entire world.

THE STORYTELLER

Years before the divorce, Wayne and Nancy moved into the house that had been the site of the famous Hobson murders. It was a Victorian-style with two upstairs bedrooms and a narrow driveway. The outside needed to be repainted, and they'd long planned on remodeling the bathroom, but in the time he lived there, Wayne always thought it was comfortable enough. The back porch was sheltered by ivy-covered lattice. Hedges lined the backyard and cellar doors opened at an angle from the base of the house. When they moved in, Wayne and Nancy hadn't known it was the Hobson house. In retrospect, Wayne knew he should've been more suspicious of the low price, but he was a person who believed himself to be incredibly clever, and at the time, he'd only understood the price as evidence of his own ability to master the housing market; he was pulling a fast one on the sellers, he'd thought, and he'd signed all of the paperwork as quickly as possible.

Wayne and Nancy first learned about the house two months after moving in, when a neighbor girl who they'd hired to babysit brought it up. "I don't mean to be rude," she'd said, "but what made you guys decide to buy the Hobson house? Didn't you know about the murders?"

Wayne and Nancy exchanged a glance. They'd heard of the Hobson case, of course, had seen the sensational reports in the local news: Mr. Hobson, the former owner, had held his wife captive, tied to a chair in the basement, where, after several days, he shot her, then turned the rifle on himself.

"I don't see why we should care about all of that," Nancy said. Everything was unpacked and they'd arranged the furniture to their liking. They'd finally begun to feel settled in the house, and the insinuation that there might be something wrong with it felt, to both of them, somewhat offensive. "People are murdered every day, all over the place. It's not so uncommon to be living where something like that's happened."

"And technically speaking," Wayne announced, "there was only one murder. One murder and one suicide. So if we're going to start talking about ghosts or something, let's at least get the facts straight. I mean, if you just think," he went on, "about how long human beings have populated the earth and how many people have been murdered in that time. World War II. I mean, the Crusades, for Christ's sake. There's probably not a spot of dirt on the whole planet where someone hasn't been murdered. Should we all tiptoe around, avoiding every single place where a person was killed?" He leaned forward, his face turning red. "It's ridiculous to me that, in spite of modern science, we have yet to stamp out this sort of idiotic superstition." Whenever Wayne got hold of an argument, it became nearly impossible for him to let it go. He and Nancy bickered constantly, though Wayne never felt that their arguments were any worse than the sort he assumed all married couples must have. He was a person who loved to criticize, who enjoyed arguing on some primal level. His conversations often devolved into lectures, and he felt the compulsive need to be right in situations where there was absolutely nothing at stake.

Years passed and Wayne and Nancy's knowledge of the crimes did not affect their lives in any way. Their son, Joey, who was three years old when they moved in, learned to ride his bike in the driveway of the Hobson house. Their daughter, Sam, who had been only an infant, was potty-trained in its upstairs bathroom.

It was three years after moving into the house when Wayne began to suspect Nancy was having an affair. The suspicion began as an ambiguous feeling in his gut, a sense of jealousy that had maybe always been creeping around inside of him and that gradually swelled as the months went on. She began borrowing what he thought were strange books from the library: self-help books, beginner's Spanish, dense philosophical novels by authors who Wayne had never heard of. They were things she'd never shown any prior interest in but which began to appear in little stacks on her bedside table. For dinner, she tried out adventurous new recipes that Wayne privately psychoanalyzed: did the sudden introduction of tabbouleh salad mean she was seeing a Middle Eastern man? And if so, why was she learning Spanish? Nancy came home late in the evenings, saying she'd been at yoga or had gone shopping. Once, she came home announcing she'd just redeemed a coupon for a free lesson at the shooting range.

Wayne pestered her relentlessly. "What's gotten into you? Why are you so bubbly lately? What's wrong with you?" Lying in bed at night, staring up at the ceiling, Wayne's mind pulled through images of the two of them—Nancy and the lover he was sure existed—having sex in different places around the house.

One weekend, while Nancy was visiting her mother in Albany,

Wayne decided to take action. There was a closet in the upstairs hallway with a shelf that had been broken for some time. The wood that held the shelf in place was rotted, and Wayne had resolved to fix it—something to busy himself with while Nancy was away. He was working to remove the old wood, prying the nails loose with a clawhammer, when he noticed that the back wall of the closet gave way a bit with each nail that he removed. He removed the shelf and pushed into the back wall only to discover that it was just a flimsy piece of paneling painted to resemble the rest of the closet's interior. A lazy patch job that he'd never noticed before. Behind the loosened panel was the dusty space inside the wall. Wayne got a flashlight and poked his head inside. The space ran the length of the upstairs hall, from the children's room at one end of the house to his and Nancy's room at the other.

An idea struck Wayne. He pushed the panel open as far as he could and slipped into the wall. Inside, he hammered flat the protruding nails, pawed away the cobwebs, and drilled a tiny hole so that, from within the wall, he had a limited view of the bed where he and Nancy slept. He tied a string to the closet's inside doorknob so he could pull it shut from within the passage. Behind the closet's back panel, he tucked a cache of the fancy granola bars that Nancy bought for the children's lunches and hung a small keychain flashlight from a bent nail.

On the morning after Nancy returned, while she was fixing the children breakfast, Wayne hid upstairs and called off work. He didn't say anything to Nancy about calling off. He waited until she left to drop the children off at school, then drove his own car around the block, parked, crept through the neighbors' yard, through the hedges, and into his own backyard. He entered the house through the back door and made his way once more into the closet passage, edging slowly until he was stationed at the peephole. He didn't have a good view, but he could see the dark blue of the comforter on their bed, and when Nancy returned, he could hear the sounds of her moving around the house—the thrumming of pipes while she showered, the whine of her blow dryer. He caught little glimpses of her walking around the bedroom in her towel and moisturizing her legs before dressing and going downstairs. The air inside the passage was dry. Wayne could taste dust on his lips. His knees grew tired. He wasn't sure how much time had passed and wondered how long he should wait. He regretted not having thought to stow a bottle of water inside the passage. He ate several granola bars, opening the wrappers slowly so they didn't crinkle, then letting them fall to his feet. When he finally heard Nancy leaving through the front door, he exited the passage as quickly as he could, spitting dust and cursing as he tore his pant leg on a nail that he'd neglected to hammer flat. Leaving through the back again, Wayne returned to his car and drove around the block, parking where he could see the driveway, sure he'd catch Nancy returning with her lover. But when her car reappeared a short while later and she began unloading groceries from the trunk, Wayne slammed his fists against the dashboard, angrier now over the idea that he might be wrong than he was over the possibility of his wife having an affair.

The truth, however, is that Nancy was seeing someone, and though Wayne hid twice more inside the walls during the following months, he never found any evidence of her infidelity—not until, finally, after putting the children to bed one night, Nancy asked him to sit down at the kitchen table, where she calmly made her confession, explaining that she was sorry and that she wasn't sure she'd ever loved him and that she couldn't see anything to do but get a divorce.

They agreed to split custody of the children: Wayne had them Mondays, Tuesdays, and the second and fourth weekend of every month. He moved into a one-bedroom apartment inside a six-unit complex about thirty minutes outside of the city. In the first month after the divorce, Wayne's thoughts were a running script of imaginary arguments with Nancy—demands for apologies, pleas for devotion—but without her present, there was no one upon which he could unload these arguments, and Wayne moved through his days in a state of manic preoccupation. He wandered the grocery store for over an hour only to end up at the checkout with nothing but tortilla chips and a brick of cheese. He forgot to unhook the gas pump from his car and nearly tore it loose when he drove away from the station. At night, he stayed up sipping beer and watching television, unable to sleep, unable to be alone with his thoughts. He discovered that he could get onto the roof of his building by way of an unmarked door and he made a habit of going up there at night, pacing and mumbling, staring out at the surrounding darkness. The building was flanked on either side by parallel highways, beyond which parking lots and small access roads knotted around strip malls and gas stations. From the roof, Wayne watched the highways on either side, the red brake lights disappearing in one direction like the jeweled fragments of his shattered life, white headlights rushing toward him in the other lane like the constant, oncoming uncertainty of the future. In the distance were the twinkling city lights, and he sometimes imagined he could zoom in on one of them, his old house, where he'd see Nancy standing at the window, the mysterious silhouette of her new lover looming behind her.

One night, standing on the edge of the roof, with all this running through his mind, it occurred to Wayne that he wanted to jump. The thought bubbled up with some mix of desperation and amusement. He snickered at the thought of Nancy having to deal with the guilt of his suicide. But then, shifting his weight, the toe of his shoe sent a few pebbles skittering over the edge, and he was overcome with an enormous feeling of terror. He stumbled backward, suddenly aware of the three-story distance between himself and the pavement below.

The children were staying with him that weekend and when he returned downstairs to his apartment, he found his daughter, Sam, standing in the darkened living room.

"I couldn't find you," she wept. "I thought you left. I thought you were dead."

The children hated Wayne's apartment. There was no backyard and none of their toys aside from whatever they stuffed into their backpacks each week. The apartment had come prefurnished and had the sterile look of something from a magazine, entirely without personality except for the crumpled beer cans that Wayne hurriedly cleaned up whenever the children were coming. He forbade them from playing outside—a sensible idea, he thought, considering the constant streams of high-speed traffic on the surrounding highways. There was only one bedroom and the children had no space of their own. They spent their time sprawled on the floor in front of the television, moaning and sighing.

"I hate this," Joey complained. He was seven years old, a first grader at H. W. Smith Elementary. "There's nothing to do."

"Next time, you can remember to bring something," Wayne responded.

"I wanna go home," Sam whined, and moments later, she broke into a tantrum, screaming and crying over boredom and exhaustion and the strangeness of her new life split between houses.

"Fine," Wayne shouted. "Fine." He jerked the children into their coats, crammed their shoes over their feet, and marched them outside, to the edge of the highway. Cars rushed past in violent blurs. The children whimpered. Wayne squeezed their tiny hands. He waited until there was a break in traffic, then pulled them across the highway and through the long parking lot toward the strip mall, where there was a toy store. "Pick something," he said. "Go ahead. You've won. Get yourselves some stupid toys." The children stood sobbing for a moment, then set off uncertainly down the aisles, their teary eyes roaming over the brightly colored dolls and action figures, the board games and remote-controlled cars. The cashier watched as Wayne paced the front of the store. Joey eventually came back bearing a set of walkie-talkies. Sam picked out a plastic Tyrannosaurus.

By the time they were walking back across the parking lot, the children were smiling. They raced across the highway, all three of them giggling with excitement, Wayne shouting "Go, go, go!" as a truck zoomed toward them. Back at the apartment, they ordered Chinese food and ate happily in front of the television, and later, when it was bedtime, Wayne tucked the children into the apartment's only bed, then cracked a beer and settled onto the couch. When he got up to brush his teeth, he stood at the doorway of the bedroom and watched them sleep and felt, if only for a moment, a sense of joy—or maybe just normalcy—that had long been absent from his life.

Two months after he'd moved into the apartment, Wayne received a letter from a man who identified himself as Nancy's lawyer stating that she was filing for full custody of the children. Incensed, Wayne called Nancy, demanding an explanation.

"Where should I begin?" Nancy asked. "Joey says you've been marching them back and forth across highways. Sam told me you left them alone in the middle of the night. She says she woke up in the middle of the night looking for you and that you were gone and she had no idea where you were."

"I didn't leave," Wayne huffed. "You're exaggerating. Let's at least get the facts straight. I was on the roof, Nancy. The kids were right below me."

"On the roof," Nancy said. "You were on the roof. Great. I don't even want to know why, at three in the morning, you were marching around on the roof. Anyway, it's not just that you left them alone, Wayne. You haven't even bought them beds yet. It's been, what, two months?"

"They sleep in my bed," Wayne said.

"Oh, come on. You remember how they used to complain about sharing a bed whenever we visited your parents? And Sam says you don't even keep food in the refrigerator. They're children, Wayne. You have to feed them. She says they ate pretzels for breakfast last week. I mean, you've got to be kidding. Pretzels?"

As Nancy went on, Wayne had the urge to argue. He thought about that night on the roof, about how he'd wanted to jump, about how it would have been her fault if the children spent the rest of their lives without a father. He felt certain that he hadn't actually wanted to die, that it had just been a sort of fantasy and that there was nothing in his body that had truly wanted to send him over the edge. But the feeling still lingered—the strange vulnerability, the fear of impulse—and he realized that the thought of killing himself had been on his mind with some regularity. It was something he thought about often at night, when he was alone. Now, on the phone, he felt cornered by Nancy's accusations, and with no other ground to stand on, he found himself describing that moment on the roof.

"Wait, wait, wait," Nancy said. "What do you mean, you were going to jump?"

"I mean that I'm fragile, Nance." His voice was high and pleading, but his mouth had lowered into a mocking frown. She had to sympathize, Wayne thought. After all she'd put him through. "The kids are all I've got left. If you take them from me, I don't know what will happen. I very well might kill myself."

There was a pause, as if Nancy was deciding whether or not to take him seriously. "You wouldn't," she said, finally. "You think too much of yourself."

"Nancy," Wayne said, and he was fully prepared to begin outlining all of the reasons why the possibility of his suicide should be treated with dignity and respect, but she cut him off before he could get another word in.

"Besides," she said, "if this killing yourself thing is real, then it's even worse than I thought. You should see someone, Wayne. You really should. You're in no condition to make sane judgments about the children's well-being. I mean, shouldn't you be required to take care of yourself before you can be expected to take care of other people? Anyway," she sighed, "I've already filed the paperwork. It'll take a few weeks to go through. Probably a couple months, I'm told, before they can schedule a court date. I'm assuming you want a court date? I know how you love to argue your case."

The following week, Wayne was driving home with the children when, glancing in the rearview, he noticed that Joey was flipping through a picture book of ghost stories. Wayne watched the boy trace a finger across the page, silently mouthing the words as he read.

"Ghosts, huh?" Wayne said. Joey made eye contact in the mirror, then went back to reading. "I don't suppose your mom ever told you about the ghosts in her house?"

"What ghosts?" Sam asked.

"I'm trying to concentrate," Joey said.

Wayne let out a snort. "No," he said, "I doubt she'd tell you the truth about that house. She doesn't like to tell the truth. Not until it's too late." Wayne peered into the rearview. He could tell Joey was listening; the boy stared down at his book, but his finger had stopped moving and he was no longer mouthing words. "Anyway," Wayne said, "you guys are probably too young for that story."

"I'm five!" Sam cried indignantly.

Wayne chuckled. "Some stories are too gruesome for five-year-olds. But if you really want to hear it . . ." The children were not used to their father telling stories—it wasn't something he ever did—and the novelty captured their attention. "People were killed in that house," he said. "With a gun." He paused, as if that was the end of the story, letting the children's curiosity stew before he went on. "Mom really never told you guys, huh? Well, okay. The people who owned the house before your mom and I, they were crazy. Old Man Hobson and Old Lady Hobson." Wayne tried to remember the details of the crime as he'd heard them in the news so many years ago, but he could only recall the basic facts. He wasn't someone with much imagination and he didn't have a good idea of how to piece the story together. "The neighbors say it was dark that night. There was a storm—the biggest storm you ever saw!—and the power went out in every house on the block. All the neighbors sat around with candles, listening to the storm, until they heard a scream. It was loud enough that everyone on the whole street heard it. It was Old Lady Hobson. By the time the police arrived, it was too late. Old Man Hobson had taken her down into the basement and tied her up. Then, he'd taken out his gun and . . . *Blam!* After he killed his wife," Wayne said, "Old Man Hobson sat down against that cold cement wall, pointed the gun at himself, and . . . *Blam!* The neighbors said the whole basement had to be repainted. To cover up all the blood! Old Man Hobson's been dead for years now, but his ghost is still walking around down there. He and his wife, both."

"Daddy," Sam said earnestly, "a ghost is not real."

"Are you telling me you've never heard the footsteps on the basement stairs? You've never heard the screaming and moaning that happens down there at night?"

The children were silent, frowning.

"When your mom and I were still together," Wayne said, "I used to wake up in the middle of the night and hear ghosts tramping up and down those basement stairs. Up and down, up and down. I tell ya, I'm glad I left that house. I'm glad your mom and I split up. It was probably only a matter of time before Old Man Hobson was going to get me too."

That night, as Wayne was putting the children to bed, Joey cleared his throat and asked, "Did all that stuff really happen? With the lady getting shot in our basement?"

Wayne smiled, held up one hand. "Scout's honor."

"Why did you scare me with that ghost?" Sam asked. "Can you leave the light on?"

"Don't worry," Wayne said. "The ghost is only at your mom's house. He doesn't come out here. Wouldn't know how to get here. They don't make roadmaps for ghosts. And ghosts can't drive. Why do you think I moved so far away? You're safe here. This is the safest place in the world."

The sky was overcast. Wayne was driving home after dropping the children off at Nancy's. He was almost home when he found himself suddenly pulling into the parking lot of a party supply store. He walked past the aisles of balloons and novelty party hats until he found a small shelf full of out-of-season Halloween masks. The options were limited. He selected a green rubber devil face that had a long tongue curling past yellow fangs. He paid for the mask, threw it into the back seat of his car, and drove back to the city. He parked on the block behind his old house and waited until it was dark and he knew the children would be in bed. Then, he stuffed the mask inside his coat, crept through the neighbors' backyard, crouched in the bushes, and watched the flickering light in the living room window, where he knew Nancy must be sitting in front of the TV. He walked across the lawn and peered in through the window, half-expecting to see that mysterious lover there with his arm around Nancy. But she was alone, sitting on the couch, scrolling on her phone with an index finger. As carefully as he could, Wayne climbed up the lattice and onto the roof of the back porch. His movements were slow and delicate to avoid making any noise. Huddled on the roof, he pulled the mask over his head, then inched toward the window of the children's bedroom. A light rain began to fall and the inside of the mask grew hot and moist with his breath. Through the tiny eyeholes, he couldn't make out anything in the window but his own reflection. He knocked on the window, gently. When there was no discernible movement, he knocked again, louder. A moment later, he heard the sound of his daughter screaming. Wayne made a menacing gesture with his hands, then turned and scrambled down the lattice and across the backyard. He dashed through the hedges to his car, where he ripped the mask off and cackled until he was out of breath.

The next week, when Wayne picked the children up from school, they both reported having seen Old Man Hobson at their window.

"I know it was the ghost," Sam said seriously. "Daddy, it was Old Man Hommon, I just know."

"Hobson," Wayne corrected. "Old Man Hobson."

"Dad," Joey said, "were you telling the truth? You really used to hear footsteps in the basement?"

"Oh, yeah," Wayne bellowed. "Practically every night. Footsteps in the basement. Chains rattling in the attic. One time—I swear!—I saw a giant eyeball floating around the backyard. It even blinked at me! I don't think I even told your mother about that one. I was too scared!"

In the morning, Wayne took the children to see a movie. They all shared an extra-large Coke, and in the afternoon, they took out Joey's new walkie-talkies and played hide-and-seek in the tiny apartment, Joey crouching under the bed or in the closet, whispering "warmer" or "colder" into the receiver while Wayne and Sam crept giddily from room to room.

"Why the hell did you tell them that stupid ghost story?" Nancy demanded. Wayne pressed the phone to his ear. "Do you have any idea how much trouble I've had getting them to bed at night?"

"Nancy, Nancy," Wayne clucked. "I was only being honest with them. You want me to be honest with our children, don't you? They ask me about that house and I'm going to tell the truth. A woman was murdered in that basement, Nancy. Tied to a chair and shot in the face. You remember those news stories. It's my job as their father to be honest with them. I don't know about you, but I don't want my children growing up with some false idea of the world. For Christ's sake, I don't want them thinking everything is just cream puffs and roses. I mean, if you think about it, that's probably how Old Lady Hobson landed herself in that whole situation to begin with. I'll bet she didn't want to admit to herself that something was wrong with her husband. I'll bet she didn't want to admit to what was happening right there in front of her. Not until it was too late. I don't want *my* children ending up like that."

"Wayne," Nancy pleaded, "you sound like a nutcase."

"You can take the kids away," Wayne went on, "but I won't let you shelter them. I won't let you send my Sam down a path in life that ends with her tied to a chair in a basement with some lunatic pacing around, ready to blow her brains out. Is that what you want, Nancy? Huh? Is that what you want?"

It became a bedtime routine for the children, when they stayed at Wayne's apartment, to ask about the ghosts. They developed a morbid curiosity about the violence that had occurred in their mother's basement and, wriggling beneath the blankets of the apartment's only bed, they'd kick and squirm, sitting still only after Wayne began his story.

"Did you ever see the blood that runs down the walls at midnight?" Wayne asked. "Some say that when she was dying, Old Lady Hobson thrashed around so much, her blood splattered all the way up the stairs and onto the walls.

"Did you ever hear that banging sound that happens in the basement? Your mom will tell you it's just the pipes, but that's because she's afraid of the truth. The truth is that it's the echo of the gunshot from when Old Man Hobson killed himself. It's still reverberating off the walls down there.

"Did you ever hear the laughing skull that lives in the closet downstairs? If you're real quiet, you can hear its teeth chattering. Cha-cha-cha-cha-cha!"

Wayne looked forward to telling these stories perhaps as much as the children looked forward to hearing them. By the time they were asleep each night, Wayne's imagination would already be buzzing with ideas for the next night's tale. Whenever the children were at Nancy's, he'd go up to the roof of his building and pace around, rehearsing new bits. He took a keen joy in inventing the details and he was amazed at how they seemed to appear in his mind as if from nothing.

"Old Lady Hobson," he told them, "she used to work in a pet store. She had a big pet bird that would fly all around the house. Some people say that's what finally drove Old Man Hobson over the edge. He hated that bird! But when the cops arrived, that was how they knew what had happened. The bird was the only witness to the murder, see? And it was a parrot. So when the cops got there and all they saw was blood everywhere and two dead bodies, they were confused, right? That is until the bird flew down from the rafters and started talking—he told them all about it! The bird gave them the whole play-by-play, and since Old Lady Hobson was dead and there was no one else to take care of the bird, the cops decided to put him to work. They gave him a job and he became the first ever bird detective. He's out there now, driving around, solving crimes. You wouldn't believe it!"

Wayne dropped the children off and watched from the car as they walked up the driveway toward their mother's house. When they knocked on the door, there was no answer, and the children stood at the front door, looking back at Wayne's car. He noticed that Nancy's car wasn't in the driveway, and then he looked at his phone and saw that he'd arrived almost fifteen minutes early. He walked up to the house and tested his old key. It still worked, so he let the children inside. He didn't want to leave them alone, so he thought he'd wait in the foyer until Nancy returned. The children raced upstairs, and Wayne stood alone, unsure of how to occupy this space that no longer belonged to him. He put his hands in his pockets, took them out, stuffed them back in. He noticed that the front hall had been repainted—a thin blue that covered the eggshell color it had been during the years he'd lived there. Wayne took a few steps inside and could see there was a new dishwasher in the kitchen. Another step and he could see that the furniture in the living room had been rearranged, space made for an exercise bike that now stood in one corner. Wayne walked a slow lap around the first floor, wondering over all these changes that had been made in his absence. Without thinking, he walked upstairs. He stood for a moment at the entrance of the children's room and watched them playing with action figures. Then he walked to the hall closet. In spite of the other changes that had been made to the house, the closet was as he'd left it. The shelf was still on the floor, propped against the back panel from the last time he'd entered the space behind the wall. He pushed the panel back just enough to see the shine of a granola bar wrapper that he'd left crumpled in the dark.

Wayne was halfway down the stairs when Nancy appeared in the front door.

"You're early," she said. "Why are you early? What are you doing upstairs?"

Driving home, Wayne felt something slide beneath the gas pedal. He reached down and found one of Joey's walkie-talkies. The children had been playing with them in the back seat on the way over. Wayne pulled over and searched the rest of the car, but the other walkie-talkie was nowhere to be found.

The next night, half-drunk and possessed with a giddy, panicked feeling, Wayne drove back to Nancy's house and parked on the street where he could see the children's window. He wasn't sure what sort of distance the walkie-talkies had, but they'd been expensive and he trusted that he'd be able to get through.

"Joey," he whispered in a low, guttural voice. He held the walkie-talkie close to his mouth, his breath dampening the speaker. "Jooooeeey . . . Joooooooeeeey." He waited. "I'm coming to get you," he hissed. "I'm coming." Nothing happened. "I'm coming to get you, Joooooeeey." He waited a while longer, then began to wonder what he was doing. He sat in his car, feeling desperate and foolish, suddenly hating Nancy, then hating himself for being so stupid as to think that he could scare the children away from her. He stared up at the house and felt a horrible loneliness descend upon him. His chest tightened and, for a moment, he had trouble breathing. He squeezed the walkie-talkie in his fist, banged his head on the steering wheel, punched himself in the thigh, and began to weep. Big, ugly tears. A wailing, animal sound rose from his throat.

And in the dark of the children's room, Joey and Sam sat up

in their beds, their eyes fixed on the nightstand, where the tiny red light on the walkie-talkie blinked and snippets of gurgling moans came crackling from the speaker like some tortured voice howling from beyond.

Wayne retrieved his mail from the square of metal boxes in the parking lot outside of his apartment. Sifting through the envelopes, he found he'd been issued a summons to appear in court the following month. He crumpled the letter in his hand, his gaze drifting absently across the sky and along the edge of the roof of his apartment building. He realized that, on some level, he'd never thought Nancy was serious, never thought she'd actually try to take the children.

"Tell us about the eyeball again."

"Yeah, the eyeball!"

"Okay, okay," Wayne said. He pulled the blankets up around the children's necks. "Once a year, on the anniversary of the murder, the eyeball will appear, and it will float through the entire house, starting in the basement, then up the stairs, out the back door, around the yard, circling the house and coming back through the front door, up to the second floor, toward the bedrooms. First, it turns to the left and looks into your mom's room. Then," he said, pausing for dramatic effect, "it turns to the right." Joey squirmed at the implication. Sam stared at her father with an open mouth. "Some people say Old Man Hobson was a devil worshipper, that he summoned the eyeball using black magic. But I think it's part of Old Lady Hobson's ghost—it flew out of her head when she was shot, and now, every year, on the anniversary of her death, her eyeball is doomed to look over the whole scene of the crime, floating through the entire house until it finally gets back to the basement, where she re-watches every detail of her own grisly death."

"Daddy," Sam said. "I don't want to go back to Mommy's house." Her brother kicked her gently under the blankets. "I don't like eyeballs. I want to stay here with you."

On the night before he'd pick the children up for what he knew could be the last time he'd ever see them, Wayne sat in his car outside of Nancy's house and drank a six-pack of beer, then unlaced his shoes and threw them into the back seat. He took out an old canvas gym bag that contained the rubber devil mask, the walkie-talkie, and a fog machine, which he'd purchased at the party supply store for forty dollars. He also took from the trunk an old fishing rod; at the end of the line, he'd affixed a Halloween decoration that he'd ordered from the internet—a plastic eyeball the size of a basketball that lit up with a small switch and some batteries.

There were five ways that Wayne could get in or out of the house: the front and back doors, which he knew would still open with his key; the windows of Nancy's room and the children's, both of which he could access from the roof of the back porch; and the cellar doors that opened up to the backyard. Wayne decided he should first make his way to the passage between the walls of the upstairs hall. When the children were in bed and he could see Nancy bobbing up and down on the exercise bike in the living room, Wayne crept across the lawn in his socks and climbed the lattice onto the roof. He shuffled his way along the side of the house toward Nancy's bedroom, pushed the window open, and clambered inside, leaving his gym bag and fishing rod on the roof. The upstairs hall was carpeted—without his shoes, if he stepped carefully, he could move in silence. Opening the closet, he pushed against the back panel and wormed into the secret passage. As slowly as he could, he pulled the closet door shut, then stood quiet for a long moment, listening to the sounds of the house around him. He could hear Nancy's footsteps downstairs, moving between the kitchen and living room. Wayne inched toward the children's room, then waited in the dark until he'd settled into a comfortable standing position.

Joey was on the cusp of sleep, eyes fluttering as he slipped into a dream: he and his father, digging for worms with their hands in the damp soil of the backyard. Joey could just about smell the earth when, suddenly, he was jolted awake by a loud knocking. He sat up and looked around the room. From the bed next to him, Sam screamed. The knocking seemed to be all around them, a terrifying clamor that sounded as if the very walls of the room were mounting an attack.

Downstairs, Nancy sighed and closed her eyes. When the screaming and banging didn't stop, she headed upstairs to see what the commotion was.

From inside the wall, Wayne could hear the frustrated tone of her voice, pleading for the children to get back in bed. When he heard her footsteps moving back down the staircase, Wayne edged toward the closet, slipped into the hall, and went back outside through the window in Nancy's room. The night air was cold. The shingles of the roof clung to the bottoms of his socks. The moon glowed behind a drift of clouds. Wayne took the fishing rod and made his way toward the window of the children's room.

Sam curled against her pillow, watching the shape of her brother shifting beneath his blankets on the other side of the room. The window was just above Joey's bed, and as the clouds pushed across the sky, the folds of his comforter looked like an elaborate landscape of shadowy dunes and darkened canyons. A light appeared, descending slowly into the window's rectangular frame. Sam looked up to see what she knew to be the monstrous, glowing eyeball of Old Lady Hobson hovering in the dark, peering in at her.

Nancy was halfway up the stairs again by the time Wayne made it back down the lattice. He pressed himself flat against the house and glanced up to where the light from the children's room had clicked on. The sound of their crying drifted out into the night. He left his fishing rod in the grass—he would have to remember to pick it up when he left. Then he crept along the side of the house and unlocked the back door.

"But just for fifteen minutes," he could hear Nancy saying upstairs, "and that's it." The children's feet pattered above him. Wayne ducked through the door that led to the basement, where he planned to execute one final scare before leaving safely through the cellar doors. He waited at the top of the basement stairs and listened while the children and their mother came down to the living room. He could hear Sam still sobbing as the three of them settled onto the couch.

The wooden steps groaned as Wayne descended into the

basement. The walls and floor were concrete that had been painted a pale gray. A single light bulb dangled from the web of pipes and ragged joisting overhead. Despite the apathy he'd felt about the Hobson murders when he lived in this house, Wayne found himself now, in the dark, wondering where, specifically, the crimes had happened. Had the chair where Mrs. Hobson was tied up been pushed into one of the corners? Or had Old Man Hobson arranged it more dramatically beneath the light of that one dangling bulb? And where did Old Man Hobson sit down—had he sat down?—to get comfortable in his final moments? Wayne stood, waiting for his eyes to adjust to the dark. When the shapes around him began to emerge—the concrete support beams that ran between the floor and ceiling, the hulking furnace that loomed next to the staircase—Wayne set down his gym bag and unfurled the cord of the smoke machine.

Upstairs, Nancy and the children sat in front of the television. Nancy clicked through the channel guide, looking for something that would put the children to sleep. Comedy specials, infomercials, celebrity singing contests. She settled on a nature show— tadpoles squirming their way toward becoming little froglings.

When the banging started, Nancy thought it must be her boyfriend, Cameron, at the front door. He'd promised to stop by later and she was eager to see him. Cameron traveled frequently for work, and it had been more than a week since they'd been able to find any time together. She hadn't let him meet the children yet, had wanted them to feel comfortable without Wayne before she sprung someone new on them, though there'd been nights when he came over after they were asleep and left before they woke. She was sure the children must have heard him from their bedroom upstairs. She hoped that, after everything was settled in court next week, she could finally feel comfortable introducing them.

Nancy was halfway to the door when the banging happened again. "Just five more minutes," she called to the children behind her. "Then it's back upstairs."

She paused before the door, wondering suddenly why Cameron hadn't just rung the bell or texted her. Then it came again, three loud raps: *thud, thud, thud.* Nancy looked around, expecting to see whatever it was that made the sound, before realizing that it had come from underfoot. The basement. The children appeared in the hall behind her, their faces crumpled with dread.

"I want Daddy," Sam said. Her voice was small and frightened. "I want to go to Daddy's house."

"Get back on the couch," Nancy told them. The sound came again, right beneath her: *thud, thud, thud.* "Go," she said sternly, and then she turned and walked as quickly as she could upstairs to her bedroom.

In the months since Nancy had divorced Wayne, her boyfriend Cameron—who often spent weekends hunting up north and was of the belief that all people should own and know how to operate a firearm—had convinced her to let him buy her a gun. "A single woman with two kids in the house?" he'd said. "What if something happened? How would you protect them?" At first, she'd thought the suggestion was ridiculous, but then, on one of the secret dates they'd gone on while she was still married to Wayne, Cameron had taken her to a shooting range, had helped her point and fire a pistol, and there'd been something strangely exciting about it. Maybe it was just a sense of autonomy she'd been learning to enjoy, or a sort of rebellion that she knew Wayne hated. After Wayne moved out, Nancy had found herself spending most nights sitting alone in front of the television, watching crime dramas, which, over time, began to fold themselves into her imagination. She'd turn on the television and every episode, it seemed, involved some vicious serial killer. One plot that stuck in her memory focused on a woman just like her—a single mother of two—who was raped and tormented by a masked invader. The final straw came one night when Cameron was over and the two of them were scared by a sudden racket from the basement—a set of paint cans knocked over by a raccoon that had gotten in through the cellar doors. Cameron had gone down with a flashlight and scared the animal off, but standing at the top of the stairs while he crept down there, hearing his shocked yelp when he shined the flashlight on the animal's snarling face—it had been enough to make Nancy lock the cellar doors and to convince her to let the man buy her a small pistol, which she kept hidden in a black metal case in the top drawer of her dresser, and which she found herself unlocking now for the first time.

The fog was filling up the basement, making it difficult to see. Wayne walked slowly, both arms out in front of him. He made his way toward the corner of the basement, where there was a small set of concrete steps leading up to the cellar doors.

Nancy held the gun behind her back to hide it from the children—she didn't want them any more scared than they already were. They stood anxiously in the doorway of the living room, the television flickering behind them. Nancy waved for them to return to the couch. "It's just a raccoon," she said, reassuring herself as much as the children. She opened the basement door and fog billowed forth around her ankles. The stairway leading down was a dense haze through which she could see almost nothing. She wondered if something was on fire, but there was no smell of smoke. She thought of the stories the children had recounted, the gory details of the Hobson murders, and then she put her foot on the first step, holding the gun out in front of her.

Wayne found his way to the cellar doors, but when he pushed against them, they wouldn't budge. He wondered if something was sitting on top of the doors on the other side. He pushed harder, banging against them repeatedly before realizing that the bolt on the outside was locked. He'd never known the cellar doors to be locked—another of the small changes that had occurred since he'd moved out of the house. He scrambled about on the concrete steps, pushing the doors at different angles, pressing up against them with his shoulders, feeling their edges with both hands.

Nancy was startled by the noise—something was over there, something much bigger than a raccoon. Through the fog, she could see, like a phantom, the gauzy shape of a man, hunched over, limbs moving frantically. In a panic, she raised the pistol and fired. For a split second, the light of the blast cut through the fog, and Wayne knew in that moment that he would not have jumped, no matter what happened with the children, he never would have jumped.

CRIME AND PUNISHMENT

The corrections officer sat on the bed in his son's room, cradling the boy's head as he wept.

"Oh god, oh god, please," the boy cried.

The corrections officer hadn't yet had time to change out of his uniform from work and the accoutrements that hung from his belt—baton, taser, flashlight, et cetera—jammed awkwardly between his body and the mattress.

"Oh god, Daddy, please," his son wailed. The boy was thirteen years old but his sobs seemed those of a much younger child. The corrections officer gently ran his fingers through his son's hair.

"Shh," he said. "Hush. It will be okay. We'll find some way to make this right."

Earlier that afternoon, at the county jail where he worked, the corrections officer had nearly killed a man. A prisoner, shackled at the wrists and ankles, clothed in the baggy jumpsuit of those awaiting sentencing. The corrections officer had beaten the man with his club. Two other guards on duty had joined in to assist and they had reduced the man's face to a swollen mass of bruises and broken teeth, his nostrils sucking for air as he was lifted away on a gurney. The incident had resulted in a small stack of paperwork, which the corrections officer filled out while sitting in the break room adjunctive to the warden's office. Pen in hand, he went over the events in his mind. A routine transport. A dozen men standing in line, awaiting the bus that would shuttle them to the courthouse or the federal prison or the state psychiatric hospital. The prisoner in question had refused to stand in line like the others, had shuffled about, chains clinking at his ankles, until the corrections officer shouted at him. And then later, when they were all boarding the bus, the man had refused to move when the corrections officer commanded him to move.

"Can't you hear?" the corrections officer had shouted. "I said *move.*"

With a grimace, the prisoner had raised his arms up to his waist—as high as the shackles would allow—and stepped toward the corrections officer. The corrections officer acted quickly, shoving the man away with one hand and unclipping the baton from his duty belt with the other.

Maybe there was something wrong with him, the corrections officer thought as he filled out the paperwork. Maybe the prisoner was crazy. Maybe he'd been having some sort of an episode.

The corrections officer hurried through the paperwork as quickly as he could; he took no pleasure in putting his thoughts into words. Later, he drove home and it was spring and the weather was warm and he rolled the windows of his truck down and the smell of freshly cut grass came blowing through with the air and sun.

Arriving home, he found his wife standing on the front steps, talking with one of the neighbors. It was clear that they were engaged in some sort of argument. The corrections officer sat in his truck, listening while he pretended to look through the glove compartment. The problem seemed to be that the neighbor's dog was missing an eyeball.

"Your kid," the neighbor stammered, "and his goddamn BB gun."

The dog had been tied up in the yard and the camera installed in the neighbor's doorbell had, apparently, captured everything. When he got out of his truck, the corrections officer stood next to his wife, and the neighbor offered warnings and accusations—about the boy, about his upbringing, about the deeper problems that this sort of animal abuse likely indicated—all of which the corrections officer and his wife responded to by crossing their arms, nodding sympathetically, and affirming or apologizing when appropriate. What else could a person possibly say in this situation? As the neighbor spoke, the corrections officer stared just above her head, where a pair of house finches fluttered about the telephone wires. An airplane cruised slow across the blue evening. A cloud drifted by and in its lumpy, cumulus shape, the corrections officer suddenly saw the prisoner's wrecked face—orbital smashed like a pumpkin, swollen flesh closed over the eye. The corrections officer looked down again, then glanced over his shoulder at his house, where he noticed the silhouette of his son at the upstairs window.

When the neighbor finally exhausted all of what she needed to say, she turned and walked angrily back across the street, and the corrections officer and his wife went inside and closed the door.

"Jesus," his wife said. She let out a sigh—part worry, part relief. "What the fuck." Besides promising to cover the veterinary bills, they had been lost as to how to respond to the neighbor's grievances, and the situation had been left awkward and tense, the course of action still unclear. Perhaps the neighbor would contact the police. Perhaps she would not.

"I guess I'll go deal with him," the corrections officer said. He knew some form of punishment was expected.

"Oh, Daddy," the boy wailed. His head was heavy in his father's lap. "Oh, please, god. Oh, please, Jesus, Daddy."

"Everything will be okay," the corrections officer said. As soon as he had entered his son's bedroom, the boy had burst into tears. From his window, the boy would have been able to hear the entire conversation with the neighbor and must have been anticipating his own punishment.

The corrections officer pressed his lips to the boy's hair. "It will be okay," he said again. "It bit you, right?" he said. "The dog. Say that it bit you." But the boy only went on wailing. He cried for a long time. The corrections officer thought that, to anyone walking past the house, it must sound as if the boy were being savagely abused. "It will be okay," he said again. "It will be okay."

When the boy had finally exhausted himself, he lifted his head and sat hunched on the edge of the mattress. Snot bubbled from his nose and lips. His eyes were huge and puffy. His face was bloated from tears, pink and wet and shining. The corrections officer put an arm around his son and drew the boy close. He kissed the top of the boy's head again, held him for a while longer, then stood and left the room. Some time later, after it was dark, the boy came downstairs. They sat together in front of the television and ate their dinner.

HAND-ME-DOWNS

My mother tells me, "You look just like your sister." She hasn't touched her food and has just stared at me all through dinner.

My sister, Anna, was abducted from our house nine years ago. She was seven. At the time, I was only in kindergarten, the younger sister, four years old.

"Jesus, Anna," my mother says.

And I reply, "Jesus, Mom."

My father shoots me a look that means *Don't*, so I bite my tongue and stare down at my food. Most nights, I would be heating up canned soup or making scrambled eggs for myself, but tonight, my father cooked chicken with balsamic glaze, asparagus, and mashed potatoes. Mom has not been doing well lately, and I can tell he's doing his best to pull us together.

My mother starts crying, and for a few moments, my father just pushes the food around on his plate. Then he sets down his fork and stands up. He helps my mother to her feet and walks her down the hall to their bedroom. I can hear his voice—patient, hushed—beneath her sobs. In a few minutes, it's quiet. I finish my plate and wait until I hear the sound of my father coming back out and turning on the television in the living room. Then I scrape the leftovers into the trash and sit down on the couch, where he and I watch the news. There's a story about a car accident on 690 and another about a stabbing downtown. It's dark outside and the light from the television changes color on my father's face. He watches the news twice every night: first, when he gets home from work at six, and then again at ten. Part of him, I think, is still expecting to hear something about my sister.

After a while, staring at the television gives me a headache. I close my eyes and lie on the couch. Soon, I hear my father's breath slow and deepen, and that's how we fall asleep.

I shower in the morning and get changed in the bathroom while my parents are waking up. I don't really have my own room because my room was also Anna's room and my mother gets upset whenever I go in there. She never says anything about it, but if I'm in there, she always comes in, too, and starts straightening the sheets on the bunk beds, dusting the shelves, or doing some other pointless chore that will keep me from being alone. She sleeps in there most nights. Anna's things are mostly still there. Her stuffed animals. Little pink clothes still hanging in the closet. In the past nine years, only the window that was broken by her abductor has been replaced.

I have my own nooks around the rest of the house—the cabinet under the television, the bookshelf in the living room—where I keep most of my stuff. Books, drawings, CDs. I keep valuable things—like the postcard that I have from when my father and I went to Niagara Falls and the photograph of my mother reading to me and Anna at our aunt's house on Christmas when I was little—in the bottom drawer of my father's tool desk in the garage. Nobody ever fixes anything, so nobody ever has reason to look in those drawers.

Before I leave for school, I creep into my room—Anna's room. I take a couple of the Barbies from Anna's old dollhouse, pull their clothes off, spread their legs, and place them atop their tiny plastic bed.

After lunch, I skip out with my friends. Darcy lives near school and her parents both work so she and Sara and I walk to her house. Darcy has some pot that a boy gave her. We smoke on the back porch and the two of them talk about the guys they want to hook up with, specifically Tim Callahan.

"I mean, Jesse Kramer is cute," Sara says, "but Tim Callahan is *hot*. There's a difference."

"You know you would kill to make out with him," Darcy says to me.

"Sure," I say, and the two of them go on talking.

My father is still at work when I get home. The door of my parents' room is closed. I assume my mother is in there napping because that's all she really ever does.

I go into my room—Anna's room—and lie down on the lower bunk. Anna's bed. The Barbies in the dollhouse, I notice, are fully clothed again, sitting across from each other in the tiny plastic kitchen. I'm still kind of stoned and I'm not sure how long I'm lying there before I'm asleep.

My dream: a hulking shadow moves across the light from the window. Long arms with gloved hands stretch across the room, touching my clothes, my hair.

I wake up when my father gets home. In the kitchen, he takes off the red vest with his name tag and hangs it on the coat rack. My father works at the pharmacy down the street. When I was younger, he had a job as a sales rep. The night Anna disappeared, he had taken me with him on a business trip to Buffalo. We spent a day at Niagara Falls, riding the Maid of the Mist. I barely remember it, but I know that I loved the roar of the falls and the feel of looking over the railing into the crashing water below. After everything with Anna, my father left his job and doesn't go away on business anymore.

He lies down on the couch and pulls a blanket over his head. There's the sound of him taking a deep breath, a small crater forming in the blanket where his mouth is.

"Hi, Dad," I say. "How was work?"

No response. For a long time, he is still. When he finally pulls the blanket away, his eyes are closed tight, and when he opens them, he stares up at the ceiling, as if he can see straight through to the sky. He takes another deep breath, then stands up, goes to his room to change. Then he goes to the bathroom. Then he pokes his head into the garage, and then he comes back through the kitchen and looks out the window to the backyard. Then he looks in Anna's room.

"Where's Mom?" he asks.

We hop in the car and drive slowly through the neighborhood. It's just after six o'clock and the sky looks like rainbow sherbet, a huge swirl of pink, orange, and green.

"Did you see her at all after you got home?" my father asks.

"I don't know," I tell him. "Your bedroom door was closed. I thought she was taking a nap or something."

We drive past the plaza where the pharmacy is, the liquor store, the park. We go as far as the high school, then turn around in the parking lot and head in the other direction. The sky grows dark, and my father turns on the headlights. The first time this happened, two or three years ago, my father found her wandering through a neighbors' backyard at three in the morning. Another time, the police brought her home after she'd been trying to wave down cars in the middle of South Avenue. About a month ago, we lost track of her at the mall and found her in the toy store, hugging a pair of confused little kids.

We drive through the quiet side streets. A group of kids walking in the road splits and regroups as we pass. An old woman waves a flashlight from her porch and calls out for some lost pet. I think maybe one of us should have stayed home and called around in case anyone has seen her, but then I try to think of who I would call and can't come up with anyone except Darcy, who has never even met my mother.

Finally, we spot her. She's pacing up and down the bottom of the highway ramp off East Colvin. A car speeds past, and she chases it a few steps, then stops and goes back to pacing.

We pull over on the shoulder and my father gets out, runs toward her without bothering to close the door. A car driving by honks and swerves. When she notices my father, my mother turns away and starts walking quickly up the ramp, but he grabs her by the arm and holds her fast. I lean across the driver's seat and close his door.

The headlights shine on them, and I watch through the windshield like it's a giant television screen. I can't hear anything they're saying. My father is pleading, and my mother's mouth is open, screaming or crying, but there's only the sound of engines as cars accelerate past us toward the highway. When she finally stops, my father puts his arms around her, and she shrinks against him. They hold each other like that for a few moments before he walks her back down the ramp. He opens the rear passenger door and my mother climbs in behind me. When traffic is clear, my father slams the gas, pulls a U-turn down the ramp, and drives us home.

Darcy and Sara drag me to the school dance. I've got nothing to wear so Darcy lets me borrow one of her dresses, which is too tight in the chest but fits me otherwise. She and Sara agree, "You look hot."

The dance is boring and after half an hour, Darcy decides we're leaving to hang out with the boys at Kevin McDonald's house. His parents are out of town and the house is empty. We walk in a pack through the rain: me, Darcy, Sara, Kevin, Jesse Kramer, Andy D'Angelo, Keith Martin, and Tim Callahan. Light reflecting from the streetlamps explodes as we splash through puddles. When we get to Kevin's house, he and Jesse decide we're going to play truth or dare. We sit in a circle on the kitchen floor, dripping with rain. Legs out in front of me, I adjust and readjust Darcy's dress.

Darcy goes first and Kevin dares me and her to kiss for ten seconds.

"On the mouth," he says. "With tongue."

We do. The boys all lean forward to watch. It's painfully obvious, the reason we are here.

Jesse Kramer picks truth and Kevin asks him how long his dick is. Everyone groans when he says ten inches.

"Swear to God," Jesse says. "Swear to God."

On my turn, I pick truth, and Andy D'Angelo asks who in the room I would most like to make out with. The boys all shift in their seats. I look to Darcy and she raises an eyebrow. She and Sara both give me a look that means *Duh.*

"I guess Tim," I say.

Tim smiles, looks away, tries to act nonchalant.

We go around the circle a few more times. Keith lights some pot and we all share three cans of beer from the fridge. Soon, everyone is either too stoned or uncreative to come up with anything very exciting. Sara claims to have a new boyfriend from another school and refuses to perform any lewd dares. Darcy undoes her bra and flashes everyone, but only agrees to do it from outside, through the window. She stands at the far end of the back lawn and we all huddle together, faces pressed against the glass. The front of her dress goes down and back up in less than a second and the window is too foggy and streaked with rain to really even see anything.

Kevin tries to convince us that we should stay the night.

"There's plenty of space," he says, "and my parents won't be home until sometime tomorrow afternoon." Tim Callahan is staying and so Darcy says she is staying too. She calls her parents and tells them she's sleeping over at Sara's house. "Come on," Kevin says. "I can see if my brother can buy us some more beer."

"I've got to be home," I tell them, and am thankful when Sara says that her dad can pick us up at ten.

My father is on the couch when I get back. The television is on. I sit down next to him and he doesn't say anything. I can't tell if he's awake or not. I don't remember at what point we both started sleeping on the couch. I suppose around the same time my mother started sleeping in Anna's bed. I curl up next to him and he puts his arm around me. The news is on, and I fall asleep to the lullaby chatter about house fires and child molesters.

We wake to the sound of shouting. Our neighbors are college

kids and they are throwing a party, the bass from loud dance music humming through the walls of their house and out into the night. From our front door, my father and I watch my mother stomping across the lawn toward a crowd of students who are gathered on their porch.

"I know what you're doing," she shouts at them, light catching the blade of the long kitchen knife that she clenches in one fist. "I know what you're up to. You can't fool me. I'll cut any one of you—and I mean any one of you—who tries to come into my house again." She wears only a thin nightgown that hangs loose on her small frame. Her voice is shrill over the commotion of the party.

My father walks calmly down the steps of our porch and out across the lawn. My mother doesn't see him at first and the moment his hand touches her shoulder, she turns fast, the knife catching his palm. He cries out, comes running back to our house holding the one hand in the other. Little patters of blood follow him across the linoleum.

"Not as bad as it looks," he says, wincing. He picks up the kitchen phone and dials 911. "For her, not me." He offers a weak smile and mashes a wad of paper towels into his bleeding palm, squeezing his wrist above the wound while he cradles the phone between his shoulder and his ear.

Outside, the college kids are yelling at my mother and at each other, some of the drunker ones egging her on, being held back by the few who are more sober and composed. A group of them have descended the steps of their porch and stand on the lawn, a loose circle forming around her. I watch a can of beer arc from the crowd and land in the grass at her feet.

It's still unclear whether my mother has actually hurt anyone aside from my father, who runs back outside holding a fistful of bloody paper towels.

I watch my mother fall to her knees and lift the knife above her head. She plunges the blade into the ground, turns up a clod of earth. She lifts the knife again, shuffles backwards on her knees, stabbing at the ground, scraping a line between our house and the neighbors'. She's muttering to herself and occasionally looking up to bark paranoid accusations at the crowd of onlookers. The music from the party is off now and everyone is just watching.

I walk across the lawn and sit down a few feet away from her on our side of the line.

"Mom," I say. "Mom, come on."

She looks up. When she sees me, she lowers the knife, the blade trembling in her fist. "Anna," she says.

I crawl closer, wrap my hand around hers, easing the knife to the ground.

"Anna?" she says again, and with her free hand, she grabs me by the arm, clutches hard, like she's holding onto the edge of a cliff. Her hands are covered in dirt. I'm still in Darcy's dress, my bare knees pressing into the cold tracts of upturned soil.

"It's me," I say. I put my arms around her and manage to slip the knife from her hands, toss it into the grass. She cries and tells me they were in the backyard, that they were whispering, that they were going to come into our house and take me away. "I won't let them," she tells me. "I won't let them." She's squeezing my arm so hard that I lose feeling.

The police arrive and so do the ambulance and the fire department. All of them speaking in loud voices, asking her if she knows where she is, what day of the week is it. How many quarters are in a dollar? Can she name the current president? They help her onto a stretcher and buckle her down, strap a hissing oxygen mask over her face. At first, she refuses to let go of my arm, flexing against the straps like Frankenstein's monster. But then the paramedics are between us, loading her into the back of the truck, standing over her so that I can't see anything. Windows all down the block are illuminated. Curious neighbors standing in lawns, drunk kids shuffling about in the flashing lights.

My father is speaking with the two cops. He nods his head yes and no and gives quiet, one-word answers. I stand next to him, and he puts his good hand around my shoulder, squeezes the paper towels with his other.

The ambulance leaves. In a few minutes, the fire department follows, and then it's just the two cops jotting down information from my father. In a few more minutes, they leave, and it's just us and the clusters of students who are still standing around, talking loudly about how crazy this all is. One of them approaches us and shyly asks, "Is she going to be okay?"

My father nods. I wonder, do they mean my mother, or me?

"It was just a couple of us standing outside for a smoke," the student says. "I guess we were sort of on your side of the lawn. I didn't think," he starts, but my father shakes his head, holds up his good hand, tells the kid not to worry about it.

"Do you want to go to the hospital?" my father asks me. "To see her? I mean, are you all right?"

I don't know the answer to either of those questions. I bite my lip, imagine what she'll look like, drugged, tubes running from her, my sister's name still hanging on her lips.

"You don't have to," he says. "Stay here. I'll go. It's late. Stay here and get some sleep. I'll drive up and figure out what's going on. I'll be back soon, I promise." He stands there for a long moment and then I put my arms around him and we hug.

"Have them look at your hand," I tell him.

He gets in the car, starts the engine. I find the knife in the grass and take it inside, wash it, put it back in the drawer. The headlights from his car are still shining through the shutters after I've settled under the blankets on the couch. I turn the television on, mute the volume and listen until I hear the tires roll down the driveway, the engine accelerating and fading into the night.

The next day, during lunch, Tim Callahan asks if I want to hang out after school. We meet in the parking lot and head toward my house. We make small talk. He says a few things about sports and movies. I nod and agree.

"Do you think Jesse Kramer really has ten inches?" I ask after a long silence.

Tim laughs. "I don't know," he says. "I doubt it."

We get to my house and no one is there. I peek into my parents' bedroom to make sure. My father is still at work. Or the hospital. I have no idea. Tim and I sit down on the couch and watch television, and I try to remember the last time there was a guest in our house.

"Can I see your room?" Tim asks.

My mouth goes dry. My voice gets lost in my throat. I take his hand and lead him down the hall. The door creaks. Sun is pouring in through the window. We sit on Anna's bed. Tim looks around at the plastic doll house on the dresser, the basket of stuffed animals in the corner.

"Do you have a little sister?" he asks.

I shake my head. "I'm an only child," I tell him.

He stares at me for a moment, then says, "I'm tired," and we lie down. He's taller than me and my head only comes up to his shoulder. He rolls toward me, stretches his arm so that his hand rests in the small of my back. I reach across his stomach, move my fingertips gently over the fabric of his shirt, and soon, our hands are moving up and down each other's bodies, slow, the room full of the sound of our breathing. I look up and his eyes are closed, his breath coming out in big, heavy gusts. We kiss each other's necks and shoulders, and then mouths, our tongues prodding around strangely against each other's teeth and the insides of our cheeks.

Tim opens his eyes. "I like you," he says.

I smile. "I like you too," I say. And then I ask, "Will you do something for me?"

"Anything."

"Stand up, just for a moment? Over by the wall." I point. "Just stand in front of the window for a moment."

He sits up. "Sure," he says. "How come?" He straightens his clothes and gets up from the bed.

"I want to see something," I say. "Just for one moment."

"Here?"

"Yeah."

He stands there, smiling, confused. He isn't hot, I think. He's just a goofy teenager.

"What now?" he asks.

I lie back in Anna's bed. I squint my eyes so that all I can see is the sun and Tim's dark figure silhouetted in the window.

"Put your arms out," I tell him. "Reach toward me."

He does.

"What are you doing?" he chuckles.

I squint harder and his fingers thin and disappear in the light. I can't see his face. I can't see anything. Only the vague and dark shape of him in the window, arms outstretched, reaching toward me, wanting me.

HOW I CAME TO SEE
THE WORLD

Even before he cleaned up, back when he spent most nights shivering in his basement apartment or nodding off at the bar, even then, T-Bone had been a lover of animals, had refused to kill the cockroaches that shared his kitchen, would crouch on the corners downtown and coax pigeons to eat from his hand. And there was that old dog he had, Marty, that was always getting hit by cars. T-Bone loved that dog. I suppose that if anyone was going to keep a pet skunk, it made sense that it would be him.

His name wasn't really T-Bone, but the nickname had been around for as long as I'd known him. His nose had collapsed from all the junk he'd snorted—at least, that's what we all assumed. The whole bridge was receded, nostrils puckered shut, so that it looked like he had a big dent in the middle, like the side of a car after a T-Bone collision. In fact, that was one of the explanations he gave to people who didn't know him well. "I was in an accident," he'd say, or sometimes just, "I had an accident," like a little kid who'd wet his pants.

T-Bone and I were living in a halfway house on the north

side of Pittsburgh. He had been locked up for a few months and got out around the same time that I left the hospital. Our rooms were across the hall from one another, and he was doing okay as far as I could tell. But the whole process of getting clean had scraped him hollow and left him searching for purpose in every stupid, meaningless thing. He bothered me with horoscopes from the newspaper, would pick up things from the ground—a mitten that had been dropped in the gutter or those pamphlets that religious groups hand out on corners—and take them home, study them as if they held some secret meaning he had to decode. He checked out books on numerology and ancient Egypt from the library and was always giving me lectures or reading me passages out loud in front of strangers on the bus. None of it ever stuck, though. He'd bounce from one thing to the next, never giving any of it enough time to sink in. Sobriety, it seemed, was the only thing he really managed to stick with.

T-Bone was so self-conscious about his nose that, even if the temperature was in the eighties, he'd sometimes pull a ski mask over his head before leaving the house. He went through these horrible cycles of depression, would push his cot against the door of his room and barricade himself inside until me or one of the other guys banged on his door, and we'd hear him croak, "Go away" or "Leave me alone," and we'd keep banging until he got fed up or someone fetched the ladder and climbed in through his window.

But other times, he walked around like Dick Van Dyke in *Mary Poppins*, smelling flowers and waving hello to everyone he passed, dancing little jigs that made me look around and pretend I didn't know him. His teeth were huge and crooked and far apart, and he had this open-mouthed grin that was almost horrifying, especially when he was wearing that ski mask. It was like someone flipped a switch, the way his moods struck. Some of the guys at the house were nervous that T-Bone was too manic, that he'd relapse, or worse, that he'd end up killing himself, that we'd kick open his door one day and find him with a belt around his neck. But one night, not long after I'd moved into the house, T-Bone found me sitting on the floor in the bathroom, pinching a blade I'd snapped loose from a disposable razor, and without saying anything else, he told me how his older sister had hanged herself when he was a kid. He'd been carrying that pain around his whole life and couldn't imagine putting another person through anything like it.

We went to recovery meetings two nights a week, and on Saturday mornings, everyone volunteered at a Methodist church, where the staff director of the halfway house was sometimes able to get us donations of canned food or toiletries. T-Bone spent the rest of his weekends sitting in a plastic booth, pressing the button that lifted the mechanical arm to allow cars in and out of a parking garage. On Tuesday and Thursday mornings, I waxed floors downtown at the convention center. I'd been at the house for almost two months and was feeling ready to leave, just as soon as I could save some money. I wanted to get out of Pittsburgh, head west and make a new life for myself. My older brother, who I barely knew, owned a restaurant franchise out in Arizona. He had written me when I was in the hospital saying that if I could get out there, he'd give me a job and let me stay at his place free of charge, at least for a while.

T-Bone and I were both trying to find more stable jobs, but in the meantime, we supplemented our paychecks by participating in medical research studies at the university hospital. Some of the nurses knew us by name. They liked us because we were reliable—we needed the money and signed up for as many studies as we could. We were regulars to the women who ran the ragweed allergy experiments. Sometimes it almost felt like a real job—waking up in the morning, riding the bus downtown, keeping track of our different appointments. It felt good to have those responsibilities. Once in a while, we could make extra cash donating platelets or blood plasma. If one of us had a particularly harrowing session, like the muscle tissue study, or the one that took anal swabs for HIV research, we'd treat ourselves to hamburgers on the way home.

Rumors always circulated about these mythical jackpot studies in which they paid you a thousand bucks, put you up in a hotel, injected you with some weird virus, and observed you for a week or so. Maybe they pumped you full of some experimental medication and maybe you were the one guy in a million who exhibited the hideous side effects, but T-Bone and I knew we had seen worse things in our lives, and sometimes we found ourselves wasting whole afternoons, dreaming about hotel jacuzzis, cable television, continental breakfasts, and big, warm hotel beds. But mostly, we talked about leaving Pittsburgh, about the other places we might go and the other lives we might live. I had decided that if I ever landed a jackpot like that, even half the cash could get me a bus ticket out to Phoenix. Setting goals was something T-Bone and I were both trying to be better at.

But our options were always limited. Because of our pasts, we often couldn't be considered "healthy controls." Plus, T-Bone was pretty much blackballed from any of the psychiatric studies. Many of the screenings weren't more than a short interview or a few boxes checked off on whatever paperwork, and we knew we could get past them easily if we lied, but honesty was another thing we were both trying to be better at.

But about the skunk.

I was doing a neuroscience study that took up my evenings and had been skipping meetings and getting home after curfew. By that time, I'd been around long enough that the staff at the halfway house left me alone, just so long as I was making money and was able to check in with them from one of the hospital pay phones. It had been a few days since I'd seen T-Bone, and I spent those days riding the bus by myself, smoking cigarettes outside with the nurses. For the study, I had to sit in front of a computer in a dark room with electrodes stuck to my head, memorizing pairs of words that were randomly generated on the screen: *Mother, Hatchet. Forest, Blinking.* After a few hours, the administrators would come in and quiz me. I knew the pairings were arbitrary, but some of them struck me as funny or strangely beautiful, and I couldn't help but wonder about them. *Umbrella, Children. Shaking, Brail.* Even after I'd signed the waivers and had everything explained, I was never exactly sure what the study was trying to prove.

I got home late after one of these sessions and a small crowd was gathered outside of T-Bone's door, debating in hushed voices how long it had been since he'd come out. Two days, three days. None of the doors had locks, but there was a trust rule—only staff could go into someone else's room without permission. I pushed through the crowd, knocked a couple of times, then peeked under the door to see if it was barricaded. I had a clear view, straight across the dusty floor. When staff finally arrived, we all sighed with a mix of relief and disappointment when they opened the door and revealed nothing more than an empty room. A note scribbled in pencil and left on T-Bone's cot explained that he was staying in a hotel downtown for a week and could we please not touch any of his belongings. A couple of the guys chuckled at this—the only things in the room were a few old phone books and some literature from Narcotics Anonymous. At the end of the note, he'd scribbled the address of the hotel and his room number—*in case of emergency.*

The next evening, I rode the bus downtown to T-Bone's hotel, wondering if we would finally live the big jackpot dream we had shared so many times.

The smell hit me as soon as I turned down the hall toward his room.

"What smell?" T-Bone asked when he answered the door. He held the door open only a crack so that I could just see his one eyeball peering out above the chain lock. Behind him, the room was dark. "Does it smell?"

Sometimes I forgot about that nose of his.

"I'm not supposed to have visitors," he said.

"Never mind that," I told him. "I came all the way down here to see you."

A housekeeper pushed a cart full of linens toward us. She waved one hand in front of her face and looked around as if she expected to see a putrid cloud floating through the air above. T-Bone closed the door as she approached and I stood against the wall, waited until she had rounded the corner, then turned and knocked on the door again.

"Come on," I hissed.

T-Bone let out a few wet coughs while he undid the chain. The door swung open, and he stood in the stretched-out rectangle of light from the hall, wearing nothing but a pair of saggy briefs. The television flickered in the darkness behind him, illuminating the edges of his tall, pale body.

I gave him a hug. "Hey," I said, "jackpot! I never thought—not in a million years. How much are they paying you?" I groped for a light switch, flicked it on, and caught a brief vision of the room: empty pizza boxes and fast-food garbage strewn all over the floor, soiled towels hanging from practically every surface, and what looked like dozens of crumpled pages ripped from a spiral notebook, covered in T-Bone's jagged handwriting and scattered about like fallen leaves. And then: a skunk waddled through the garbage, lifted its nose, sniffed the air, and disappeared under the bed.

I laughed—I couldn't help myself—not a joyful laugh, but an involuntary, nervous laugh. T-Bone closed the door. He sneezed and wiped his nose with a fistful of toilet paper, then fastened the locks on the door. He flicked the lights back off, returning the room to darkness. "Keep it off," he said. "She's nocturnal."

I stood there blinking while my eyes adjusted, waiting to spot the skunk whenever it crawled back out. In the dark, I could see that the bed had been stripped down to the bare mattress and the bottom drawer of the dresser was pulled out and lined with rumpled bedsheets. I coughed against the thick odor of the skunk. A sitcom laugh track growled from the television and the skunk emerged again, its tail like a frayed rope, nose in a pile of trash. It sniffed around, then lifted a leg and pissed on the carpet.

"I've got it all worked out," T-Bone said. "We'll go to Arizona, just like you've been talking about. I'm going to buy a cabin. I want to just live out in nature, you know? Out in the desert. Be among the animals. Yesterday morning," he explained, "I leaned out the window for a cigarette and there she was." He nodded at the skunk. "Two of them! She and her sister—God bless, rest in peace." He bowed his head and made the sign of the cross. "I climbed out and followed, watched them chase each other around the dumpsters and out across the parking lot, and then they were going across the street, and from nowhere, a truck—a real nut, that driver—he comes down and *whoosh*." T-Bone mimicked the impact, slapping the heel of his palm into the cup of his other hand. "Terrible. I scooped this little one up just before another car came past." He shook his head in disgust. "She put up a fight, you know, scratching and spraying, but I wasn't about to just leave her out there all alone with her family squashed in the road like that. Nuh-uh. No way." T-Bone crossed the room, crouched, and ran his hand through the white stripes along the skunk's back. I could see now that his chest and arms were decorated with long pink scratches—proof of the whole encounter.

"I named her Cindy," he said, and his mouth curled into that enormous grin.

"P.U.," I said. "I think I'm gonna be sick." I stepped past T-Bone, pulled the cord on the ceiling fan, pushed the window open, and let a cold breeze enter the room. I sat on the edge of the mattress and looked out the window. The bright reflection of television was superimposed over the parking lot outside, a current of headlights pulling fast along the street beyond. The skunk sniffed a wide circle around the bed, and I pulled my feet up onto the mattress so that it couldn't get near me. There was something unsettling about the way the skunk was walking around with nowhere to go. She looked exactly like a wild animal trapped in a hotel room.

I looked at T-Bone. His chin glistened in the light from the television. "Dude, you're drooling," I said.

He turned away, wiped his face with the wad of toilet paper that was still in his hand. His smile disappeared. "It's the medication," he snorted. "They said it increases my glands. You know, my saliva glands. Whatever." He lifted the animal in his arms and placed her in the dresser drawer, which I realized was meant to be a little, skunk-sized bed.

There was a knock at the door and T-Bone coughed and sneezed, then leapt to his feet and hustled me into the bathroom.

"Just keep quiet," he whispered. He closed the bathroom door and I stood alone in the dark. A moment later, the door swung open again and he plopped the skunk—still swaddled in bedsheets—into the bathtub. I pressed my back against the wall and listened to T-Bone greeting someone in the other room. The two of them spoke in low voices. I tried to breathe through my mouth, but I could taste the skunk as much as I could smell it. Being so close to a wild animal, trapped with it in that small, dark bathroom—my stomach tightened, as if it were being lifted on a hook toward my throat. The skunk scratched against the porcelain and then slid down over the side of the tub, its claws tapping on the tile floor. My fingers found the top of the toilet and I lifted one foot to stand on the rim of the bowl. A soft brush of fur moved against my pant leg and despite every horrible thing that I have witnessed in my life, despite all the times I have hurt the people I've loved, despite the times I stood in front of the mirror and smiled at my own death, when I felt that animal move past me in the dark, I put one hand over my mouth and screamed.

In the same moment, the bathroom door flew open and T-Bone shouted, "All clear!" and I was so surprised that I slipped and plunged my foot directly into the open bowl of the toilet.

T-Bone sat on the side of the tub. He held a clipboard tucked under one arm and with his other, he lifted the skunk onto his lap. I planted my dribbling shoe on the bath mat. Cigarette butts swirled around the toilet water in my wake.

"Nothing to worry about," T-Bone said. "Just the nightly checkup." He scribbled on the clipboard. "Records of my symptoms. They'll come back for it in the morning, look me over, take a blood sample, shine a light down my throat and tell me what's inside. Other than that, they basically leave me alone in here. Now, let's see . . ." Then he orated, speaking each word aloud as he wrote: "*I. Feel. Oh. Kay.*" He glanced at me, then back down at his clipboard. "*No. More. Drool.*" I kicked off my shoe, peeled away the damp sock. The skunk sniffed at the end of T-Bone's pen. I must have been making a face because T-Bone looked at me and said, "I'm taking care of her, okay? Just worry about your own self." He set the animal down in the tub and resumed scribbling. In another moment, he stood up and threw an arm around my shoulder. "You brought your swim trunks, right?"

I'll be the first to admit that there are a lot of things I never learned how to do. My father died when I was a baby and, relatively speaking, I wasn't much older when I dropped out of school. I've mostly worked at pizza shops and gas stations since then. I'm no good on computers and I probably couldn't point to any countries on a map aside from the United States or Canada, and despite all our talk about the hotel dream, I had always been too embarrassed to admit to T-Bone that I never learned how to swim.

I had thrown a pair of cutoffs into my backpack, but I had mostly been excited for the possibility of sitting around in a bubbling jacuzzi. As it turned out, the hotel didn't even have a jacuzzi.

The air in the pool area was thin with a chemical pungency, but it was a welcome change from the room with the skunk. The water was empty aside from the two of us and while T-Bone did jack-knives off the diving board, I walked back and forth in the shallow end and watched the shape of my body ripple and distort beneath the surface. It was strange and comforting to feel my limbs pushing through the water, the difficulty of planting my feet firmly on the bottom. I remembered one of the word pairings from the neuroscience study: *Tethered, Blur.*

T-Bone splashed toward me from the deep end. He didn't ask whether or not I could swim, just smiled and sputtered and said, "Watch me. Like this. Keep on kicking. And cup your hands."

I did as he said, splashing everywhere and not making any forward progress.

"You're a natural," he said.

A boy and girl, nine or ten years old, came in and sat in the plastic chairs near the towel rack. They whispered to one another while they watched us.

"Let's get out of here," I said. T-Bone splashed a noisy circle around me. "Besides, what you're doing, that's just doggy-paddling. That's not even real swimming. Listen." I could feel those two kids watching us, probably thinking I was some loser who couldn't even put his head underwater. I wanted to leave. I wanted to make T-Bone stop everything he was doing. I cleared my throat. "I mean, really, they're not going to let you bring a skunk back to the house."

"Oh, I'm not going back," T-Bone said.

"What do you mean, you're not going back?"

He stood up and shook his head. "We're hitting the road, remember? Jackpot. I'm a big winner. We did it."

I wasn't sure what to say. I'd told T-Bone about how I was

planning to leave soon, about buying a bus ticket and getting out of here. But despite the countless times we'd shared our fantasies, I realized now that I'd never truly imagined T-Bone coming along with me.

"They already gave me a big-time check," T-Bone said, "and I get another one next week when I finish. I've got it all worked out. We'll use half of the money to rent a car—something nice, so we can leave in style. Then the other half I can use to get started on the cabin."

"Yeah," I said, crossing my arms, "the cabin. Right."

"Race you to the far side." T-Bone grinned and took a huge, gasping breath, dunked his head underwater, and splashed, inch by inch, back toward the deep end. The kids were in the water by then, jumping in and climbing out and jumping in again. The shallow side was small enough that I couldn't go anywhere without getting splashed by them. T-Bone touched the far wall, and I watched, embarrassed, while he splashed back toward me.

Fingers wrinkled and teeth chattering, we walked back through the lobby, wet footprints darkening the carpet behind us. A cart stacked with linens was parked in the hall. As I scanned the numbers on the doors, it became clear that the cart was in front of T-Bone's room. The door was open and inside, a woman dressed in the black polo and slacks of the housekeeping staff was spraying long hisses of air freshener back and forth across the room. The ceiling fan cut fast circles above her. The sheets on the bed were fresh, the comforter tucked neatly at the corners. The dresser drawer where T-Bone had made the skunk's bed was closed.

T-Bone stomped across the room and rummaged around while I stood in the doorway and scanned for any sign of the skunk. When she noticed us, the housekeeper began speaking in another language, but T-Bone paid her no attention. He pulled the drawers out from the dresser, looked under the bed, then marched into the bathroom, pulled back the shower curtain, lifted the lid of the toilet.

"What did you do with her?" T-Bone whimpered. "Oh, please, God. What have you done with Cindy?"

The housekeeper let out a string of words, gesturing at the trash that still littered the room. She gently kicked at a Styrofoam takeout container near her foot, and then, with one finger, she pushed upward on her nose and snorted like a pig. She sprayed a short hiss of air-freshener in T-Bone's general direction. We had a pretty good idea of what she was saying after that.

T-Bone looked down at his feet and raised one hand to cover his nose. The housekeeper was already headed for the door. T-Bone slammed it shut behind her and the plastic *Do Not Disturb* sign we'd neglected to put out clacked against the door.

I felt a breeze and noticed the curtains trembling in front of the open window.

"Look," I said. "She's probably fine. She's probably made her escape out the window and returned to the wild. This is good. She'll be happier out there." I gestured to the vast parking lot outside. "In nature."

T-Bone was already lacing up his shoes, pulling his ski mask over his head. He climbed up onto the windowsill and out through the window, toppling down into the hedges that ran along the side of the building and flailing around like a wind sock for a moment before crashing onto the strip of grass beyond. I grabbed a pack of cigarettes from the dresser, stuffed my feet into my shoes, and followed him out.

"Come on," T-Bone called, springing to his feet. "She can't have gotten far."

I lit a cigarette and walked slowly behind while T-Bone peeked beneath cars, getting down on his hands and knees, calling, "Cindy? You there, girl? Cindy?"

"I'll check down this way," I said, and headed off toward the far end of the parking lot. My one shoe was still damp from the toilet and a lump of guilt was hardening in my stomach—it was me who had opened the window in the first place, and I could see how it was my fault that Cindy had escaped, if that was, in fact, what had happened. At the same time, I prayed the skunk wouldn't show up. I didn't bother to check under any cars, just walked along the edge of the parking lot, past the windows of other rooms, some of them dark, and some open, lights on, the babble of television trickling out into the night, each of them filled with normal people living normal lives. My warped reflection followed me in the windshields. I reached the end of the building and sat down on the curb. The noise of traffic hummed from the street, and I thought about being out there, speeding along in a nice, clean rental car. Then I imagined the same thing, but with T-Bone sitting passenger side and the skunk curled up in back.

Later on, sitting at the kitchen table and explaining everything to the staff director at the halfway house, T-Bone would describe what happened. He would tell how he'd spotted Cindy curled up beneath a Chevy, how he'd been trying to coax her out. I could picture him down on all fours, drool running from that stupid grin, body covered in weird, pink scratches, no clothes but a ski mask and sneakers and his Hawaiian-patterned swimming trunks, reaching under the car without realizing that the windows were open, that someone had been sitting inside and was stepping out just as he was cooing, "Here, girl. Come on out here, you precious little baby girl."

I heard the sound of the woman's scream and as I jogged back across the parking lot, I could see her standing beside the car, keys and purse dangling from her hands as she delivered a number of swift kicks to T-Bone's ribs. When I got close enough, I grabbed her by the wrists and pleaded with her, told her she had it all wrong, that this wasn't what it seemed like. T-Bone was at my feet, moaning and gasping. The woman shouted for help. Footsteps clapped against the pavement behind me. From the corner of my eye, I could see two security guards and a hotel clerk in a red jacket running toward us from the lobby.

I have never spent more than the occasional night in a holding cell, but I have dealt with my share of street cops and social workers and judges who have seen promise in my future and granted leniency for my transgressions, and I knew that T-Bone and I both had files, that our names and our fingerprints belonged to the state, and that neither of us could afford much more trouble in our lives than we'd already had. I let go of the woman's wrists; she cocked her arm and clobbered me across the jaw. I stumbled backward, then I grabbed T-Bone by the arm, yanked him to his feet, and ran.

We sprinted through downtown. Cars honked and brakes squealed. T-Bone coughed and wheezed behind me, a whistling sound coming from his throat with each breath. We put a few blocks between us and the hotel, ran past the neon bars and the chain-linked construction sites, then up into the small, dark residential roads. I pulled T-Bone along. We reached the railroad tracks at the edge of the park. Our footsteps thundered as we jogged down the empty trails. We collapsed against the cold metal railing that circled a reservoir at the center of the park.

T-Bone coughed and retched. The lights from the city glowed above the treetops and ducks glided silently over the dark surface of the water, which lapped in a slow rhythm against the concrete basin. The night was warm, but I was sweating from our escape and the wind felt cold against my skin.

I listened to T-Bone wheezing for a while longer, and then I told him, "Gimme that stupid mask." I pulled it off his head and tossed it down into the water. "I'm going home," I said, and I walked away, down the path that circled the basin. We were a couple of miles from the halfway house—I was pretty sure there was another path on the far side of the reservoir that would lead through the trees and out onto the streets on the other side of the park. When I peered over my shoulder, T-Bone was gone, but then I noticed the tiny, pale shape of him moving on the opposite side of the reservoir, growing smaller and farther away. As I walked, I looked down into the water, a shimmering darkness that grew wider and wider between us. I tried to pinpoint the moment when T-Bone and I reached the widest point of the circle, when we were as far apart as we could be and were no longer walking away but heading back toward each other. Another minute and I could hear his wheezing breath again. T-Bone made it to the path on the far end before me. He headed down into the trees and jigsawed through the park, and I followed behind him. His breathing sounded worse and worse. We didn't speak, just kept going deeper into the forest. Eventually, the trail thinned and disappeared, and we were walking along the edge of a muddy stream that crept across the earth like blood from a slow wound. T-Bone pushed his way through the brush, clearing a path, and I walked behind him, keeping my distance, like a stray dog. The ground swelled into a ravine around us, and we followed the stream to where it trickled from the mouth of a metal storm pipe. We climbed the slope around the pipe, our hands grasping at roots and branches. I had no idea which direction we were headed in now, but it didn't matter. I wanted to make sure T-Bone got home okay. He could have been headed anywhere and I would have followed.

Coming over the crest of the ravine, I could see streetlights through the trees. The doors at the halfway house would be locked by now, and we would have to convince whoever was working to let us inside. We kept walking through the night, the smell of chlorine still clinging to our bodies.

T-Bone was bedridden for days. Whenever he breathed, it sounded like a big wad of bubblegum was stuck inside his lungs, stretching and squishing each time they inflated and collapsed. The skin around his nostrils became so chapped that the edges bled and scabbed. I wondered what it was they had injected him with in that hotel, and if maybe he was, in fact, that one guy out of a million who was exhibiting the hideous side effects.

In the last intelligible conversation we had, he was sitting up in bed, nibbling french fries that I'd brought him from the hospital cafeteria, and he told me about how, when he'd found Cindy beneath that car, for whatever reason, he knew that they were saying goodbye.

I woke early the next morning and went outside for a cigarette and found T-Bone pacing in the road, shivering and talking to himself. He hadn't changed his clothes all week and was still wearing those blue Hawaiian swimming trunks. The scabs on his chest from when he'd first caught the skunk were bleeding again; he'd scratched them back open. I called out to him but he didn't seem to hear anything I said. Some of the other guys from the house helped me walk him back inside and, thinking he'd relapsed, the staff had him pee in a cup, but before there were any results, two cops arrived. They put T-Bone in the back of their car and drove him downtown. Of all things, he had missed a meeting with his probation officer.

T-Bone spent a night shivering in a cell downtown before he was transferred to the hospital, where, after another day, he was diagnosed with rabies. I managed to visit him before he was moved into the infectious disease unit, and by the time I saw him, it was like someone was flicking that switch in his brain, on and off, on and off. Sitting bedside, I noticed the plastic ID bracelet around his wrist. As close as we'd been, I had never known T-Bone's real name before then. I held his hand and rotated the bracelet so that I could read it: *Jeffrey P. Brzowski*. I put my hand on his cheek, and it felt as warm as a cup of coffee. He was in the hospital for three nights before he died.

I hate to think that T-Bone's death is how I came to see the world, but I know that I never would have been able to leave while he was alive. I stayed at the halfway house for another few weeks, then bought a beat-up Honda at a police auction for less than it would've cost to bus cross-country. I drove hundreds of miles through fields of wheat and corn that shuffled in the sun and low green hills that rolled across the earth like the ripples of a huge wave before the car broke down in Colorado, outside Glenwood Springs, where I got a job washing dishes at a sports bar right off the interstate.

The weather has been mild enough that I can spend nights in the car while saving to fix whatever is busted. Most days, I work as many hours as they let me, staring down into the murky dishwater, and the whole universe is nothing but tiny yellow jewels of oil swirling around shipwrecks of wet food.

Each night, I walk back to the car with the Rocky Mountains rising behind me, black shapes against the already black sky, like a bad memory from childhood, somehow both urgent and far away. Sometimes, when I can't sleep, I gaze up through the windshield at the enormous night and try to remember those pairs of words from the neuroscience study—*Chimney, Bones. Whisper, Collection*—and I can almost begin to fool myself into thinking that there is some sort of order to the universe, that there is a reason for the way certain things are paired together, and that the reason will someday make itself known to me. But my mind always wanders back to memories of T-Bone going crazy in his hospital bed, and I can't sleep at all, remembering his dried, cracked lips and the gummy saliva clinging to the corners of his mouth.

BLINDNESS

Mark and Miriam lay in bed and pretended to be blind, eyes closed, gently touching each other's faces. It was something they had seen in a movie, maybe—a blind woman feeling someone's face, trying to imagine what that person looked like, or what expression they were making—and had become a sort of game that they played. The two of them agreed: they would each rather lose their sight than lose their hearing. Though, Miriam, with her eyes closed, running her thumb over Mark's cheek, reminded him between kisses, "Beethoven went deaf and he just got really good at *feeling*."

This pretending mostly happened at night, before they fell asleep, or in the gray of early morning, if they woke before their alarms, and often just before or after they made love. Those times, each of their hands would feel the other's face, slowly moving down over shoulders, ribs, and hips, searching one another, the soft brush of fingertips becoming more and more bold, one hand taking another and placing it—*here*, or *can you*, or *like this*—with eyes shut tight until they were panting, gasping, and sometimes,

Mark might open his eyes and watch Miriam's face, furrowed with pleasure, and if she noticed, Miriam stared back, and seeing one another like that—it was almost too much for either of them.

They had been dating for just over eight months and Mark daydreamed of proposing. He was confident that Miriam would say yes, but he also knew that it would be smarter to wait. They were young—he was twenty-seven and she was twenty-five. They had only been living together for two months. Mark knew there was no reason to rush into anything: the longest relationship he'd ever been in had lasted over four years, and it was almost as long after that before Mark began to realize how unhappy he had been through most of it. There was a nervous part of him that felt the need to outlast that timeline.

On top of that, Mark knew that it would be some time before either of them could afford even a small wedding. Mark worked part-time as a program coordinator for a local nonprofit, helping to develop a summer art program with a small community center in their neighborhood. While he hated the red tape and politics of the nonprofit world, he believed the work was noble and important. Miriam worked as a barista at a coffee chain. The work was nothing more than a paycheck to her, but she'd gone straight from high school to college to graduate school, and this was her first job in the service industry; it still held some novelty for her, and she enjoyed interacting with all of the different people that were her customers.

She and Mark both talked about trying to find new jobs, but they were relatively content with their lives, and every night, when they got into bed, they asked about each other's day, and Mark told her about any funny things that the kids at the community center had done, and Miriam told him about the eccentric customers she had served.

"Remember the man with the parrot that I told you about?" she asked one night. "He was back."

Mark rolled his eyes. "Let me guess," he said. "Yo, ho, ho and a barrel of chai. Chemex marks the spot."

"No, no," Miriam sighed. "Polly wanna latte. That's all."

"Well, did the bird tip?" Mark grumbled.

"I wouldn't think he was funny if he didn't."

Most mornings, Miriam had to open the coffee shop by seven, and she was usually out the door and on the bus by the time Mark was conscious enough to remember who and where he was. He never had to be at work until noon and he took his time each morning, reading in bed for an hour or so before brushing his teeth and getting dressed. Those mornings, even though their apartment was only three rooms—bedroom, bathroom, and a combined living room and kitchen separated by a few short feet of countertop—the space felt strangely large to him, and Mark moved through it as if he were in a museum, standing for several minutes in front the rosemary plant on the windowsill or the two small photographs of Miriam's parents that hung in plastic frames from Goodwill. The apartment was still new to them. In the living room, they had no furniture aside from a bookshelf and a small coffee table. They ate their meals sitting on the floor and spent most of the rest of their time in the bedroom, sprawled among the blankets, reading or watching movies on a laptop. Mark sometimes felt as if their lives were somehow too small and intimate to fill even the tiny space of their apartment.

"Don't you think we should move somewhere smaller?" he asked before they had signed the lease.

"Smaller?" Miriam replied. She raised her eyebrows, peered at him over her glasses. "Like what? A studio? What do you mean, smaller?"

"I don't know," Mark said. "I guess anything else would be a bit tight."

"I guess so," Miriam said.

When he imagined proposing, Mark mostly thought about how he would ask and not so much about what his and Miriam's lives might be like as a married couple afterward. He didn't know what he would say, but he imagined that it would be a short, matter-of-fact conversation—a simple scene at a booth in the diner where they sometimes went for breakfast on the weekends, or while they moved around each other in their kitchen, cooking dinner on a quiet weeknight—a small, private agreement, each of them saying *yes,* together, *yes, sure, why not,* and smiling at one another before realizing that the pasta was boiling over.

One night, after having drinks with some friends, they went for a walk on the trail that ran along the Allegheny River and Miriam asked Mark about his past relationships. With some hesitation, Mark told her the names of each of the women he had dated, how long each relationship had lasted, and what phase of his life they had each taken place during. "Amy and I were together for about a year," he said. "A little less. That was high school. My first kiss." Miriam snorted and punched him playfully on the arm. "Then I dated this girl, Katherine, for about a year. But she was going to college a couple hours away from me. Long distance. I'm surprised that lasted as long as it did. She's a pastor now. She's got like a hundred kids. And then Rachel and I were together for a little over four years." Mark shook his head. "It's funny to look back now and realize how obviously depressed I was during that whole stretch."

Mark chuckled but found himself feeling suddenly on guard. They had discussed, on just one previous occasion, his past struggles with depression, but all that Miriam knew was that Mark had been on some medication and that he was, at one point, briefly hospitalized. It was all in the past and she didn't consider it something that she needed to know about. Mark had not told her the reason for his hospitalization nor the fact that it had happened only a few weeks after Rachel had broken up with him. But he found himself now recalling that night, the gnawing hollow he'd felt in his chest and the pulsing need he'd felt all around him while he'd gotten drunk in the bedroom of the apartment he and Rachel had shared, still littered with all of the things she'd left behind—pages from magazines tacked to the wall and plants and books and hairpins cluttering the bedside table, none of which Mark had gotten rid of—and his own belongings, nearly all of which had taken on some horrible sentimental value since she'd left, each one gaining some ounce of the weight of memory and of his suddenly displaced love—before he swallowed as many different pills as he could find in the medicine cabinet, lay down in the middle of the floor, and fell asleep with no intention of ever waking up.

"What do you mean by that?" Miriam asked.

"By what?"

"You sounded like you were going to say something else."

"Oh," Mark said. "No. I mean, I don't know. I was just thinking." He took a deep breath. "I don't know." He was silent for a moment. Then, smiling, "I'm just really happy now. That's all."

A cool breeze rose from the water and tiny headlights traveled fast along the highway that stretched along the opposite bank of the river. There was the sound of a piano being played from one of the houses nearby, a song that might have sounded joyful or triumphant were it not being played by slow and clumsy fingers. Miriam squeezed Mark's hand in hers. "Me too," she said.

They walked silently for a bit before Mark asked, laughing

and pointing his finger at her accusingly, "Well, what about *your* exes?"

"There are none," Miriam teased with an affected superiority. "I was a virgin when we met," she joked, "and you're the first man I've ever known." Mark scoffed. "Hey," Miriam said, "watch yourself." She gave him a gentle shove. "None of them have very interesting stories. There was Adam and Aaron and Danny and Eric, and before that, there was Julian. Shawn and Amir, and—"

"Oh, God, come on," Mark said.

"—and Tom," she said, "and Jamie and Nathan and Ray. Come to think of it," she laughed, "I guess I have broken a few hearts. But there have really only been a couple who lasted more than a few months. Don't worry though, they've all come to relatively polite endings. Nobody has ever taken me too seriously, I suppose. Or maybe vice versa."

They came to the overpass of the 40th Street Bridge, where the train tracks ran beside the massive concrete abutment and the traffic above them echoed among the steel pile caps, and as they turned around and headed back toward their apartment, it occurred to Mark that this was the perfect moment, that he should ask Miriam to marry him. He could just make the casual suggestion and it would be fine, he thought. The fact that they didn't have any money was irrelevant. Miriam had begun to tell him about a customer she'd served earlier—a kind old man with a glass eye and a fur coat—but Mark's mind was running through variations of how he could propose and how the conversation might play out if he did. An urgency began to lump in his chest and his whole body clenched with a feeling of anxious reverie, but by the time he had cleared his mind of the echoes of those imagined conversations, Miriam was pulling him off the path and back toward the orange glow of streetlights, and in another moment, the brick face of their apartment was there in front of them and she was fumbling the keys from her pocket, rushing to unlock the door so that she could get inside to use the bathroom.

They sat on the floor in the living room and finished what was left of a bottle of wine, then sat together on the side of the bath-tub while they brushed their teeth. When Miriam stood to spit out her toothpaste, their eyes caught in the mirror. Mark laughed and bits of minty foam speckled the faucet.

They undressed and climbed into bed. Mark reached to turn off the light. He fell asleep quickly and dreamed of the apartment that he and Rachel had shared so many years ago. Somewhere in the dream was the bright light of a hospital. The chalky taste of pills. The ceiling fan cutting endless dizzy circles somewhere far above him, the floor sinking below. It was only a few minutes later that he woke to the touch of Miriam's fingers on his cheek. He blinked in the dark and rolled onto his side to face her.

Miriam's eyes were closed, her mouth slightly opened. Mark watched her face in the dark as she traced his jaw, pawed at his forehead and nose. He lifted his hand and ran a finger over her eyebrow, down her temple, along the rim of her ear. The dream faded from his mind, all of it becoming as dim as the past. Mark felt a bit drunk, and very happy, and very tired, and he couldn't help but close his eyes. They both were blind now, trying to pic-ture one another in the dark. He tucked a bit of hair behind Miriam's ear, then rested his hand on her face. He felt a pull in Miriam's cheek and knew that she was smiling. Yes, he thought, that was unmistakably a smile. His fingers moved over the tight-ened corner of her mouth, the swell of her cheek, and he won-dered, as he often did, what it was that she was thinking.

LETTERS FROM TOBY

I got a letter from Toby today. He wrote about a fight that happened between a black guy and a white supremacist. *They had both been bragging to everyone for weeks about how they were going to beat the other up,* Toby wrote. *People were betting cigarettes on who would win. We were all getting excited for it.*

Whenever a new letter from Toby arrives, I get a feeling like a brick in my stomach. My wife usually gets home from work before me and will bring the mail in. She knows the situation and doesn't say anything, just leaves it piled on the table with the bills and junk mail. I can spot one of Toby's letters from across the room, the words INMATE MAIL stamped in red ink and my name and address made out in Toby's jagged, lightning-bolt handwriting.

When they finally fought, Toby writes, *all that happened is the black guy got one or two punches in and then the guards hit them both with clubs. It was over pretty fast. Disappointing.*

I usually leave his letters on the table for three or four days before I even pick them up. Even then, I might carry one around in my backpack for a week before I read it. I'll wait until I have time alone—sitting in my car at the end of the workday or in my bedroom on a Thursday night when my wife is at her yoga class. After I read it, I'll fold the letter back into its envelope and tuck it inside the back cover of whatever book I'm reading. I usually carry it around like that again for another week or two before I sit down to write a response, and then I'll put his letter with the others: in a shoebox on the shelf in my closet where I can almost forget about them.

Toby is my second cousin—the son of my father's aunt and uncle. I've never been particularly close with my extended family, not even my first cousins, but my father's side is small, and Toby and his twin brother Luke were the closest to me in age, only a year younger. My only other cousins on that side are nine or ten years older than me, so growing up, whenever my parents and I drove from Syracuse to visit our family in Pittsburgh, I would end up running around with Toby and Luke. Their parents owned a summer home in Ocean City, New Jersey, and we used to visit there every year over Labor Day weekend.

When they sent me to Camp Hill, Toby writes, *they told me that it was one of the worst prisons because it was so violent. But it's really not bad compared to the state hospital. The people at the hospital, they were truly crazy. One time, I saw a guy try to kill someone with a plastic lunch tray. And there was another guy who I once saw eat his own feces. You wouldn't even believe it. The fights at Camp Hill are always short because the guards are so eager to jump in and beat someone up. At the hospital, the fights could last forever.*

Seven years ago, when he heard about what Toby had done, my father called me at work. It was April but the weather was still cold. I was in the middle of teaching and didn't pick up my phone. During my free period, I walked down to the teacher's lounge, where the vice principal was looking over the end-of-year exam schedules and Mrs. Young, the history teacher, was grading a pile of quizzes. I bought a Coke from the vending machine and called my dad back, not expecting that it would be about anything important.

"Your cousin Toby," my dad said. Listening to his voice, I could picture him shaking his head, biting his lip. He cleared his throat. My father has worked as a newspaper reporter for my entire life, and he has a way of delivering bad news bluntly, like a headline. "I mean, he went crazy. Listen. He killed Luke and their mom and dad."

Mrs. Young and the principal must have seen my face. When I hung up, the principal asked me what was wrong, and I repeated what my father had told me.

"Jesus," she said. "Do you need to leave? You should go home for the day. You should take bereavement."

Mrs. Young put a hand on my shoulder. "I'm sorry," she said. "God, that's awful."

"We can get Mrs. Vetnor to cover your last two periods," the principal told me. "You should go be with your family. We'll get you a sub for the rest of the week."

"No," I said. "No, it's okay. I mean, they're not," and I trailed off, let my eyes wander around the various posters and fliers tacked up on the bulletin board by the door. I didn't want to have to explain this to any of the other teachers, didn't want to explain it to my ninth graders, who would surely ask why I was out. "He's my second cousin," I said. "They're not very close relatives." It was true; at the time, it had been years since I'd spoken to Toby or his family.

I stayed at work through the rest of the day and then through the rest of the week. "Don't bottle your grief," my wife warned. "You can take some time off." She was studying for a PhD in literature and was giving a lecture at a conference that weekend, but that was just as well. I told her she didn't need to come along. On Friday, I left school as soon as the final dismissal bell rang. I drove home, packed my bag, and headed to Pittsburgh for the funeral.

When I write to Toby, I try to remember the version of him from our childhood, the version of him from those trips to Ocean City. I remember how the three of us—me, Toby, and his brother Luke—would go exploring beneath the boardwalk, where the sand was cold and damp and littered with trash that had fallen through the cracks above. We would climb the wooden support posts and stick our fingers through the boards, imagining ourselves as subterranean monsters, hoping to scare the people who walked among the surf shops and food stands above. We would try to gross out our parents by filling plastic buckets with the dead jellyfish that washed up on shore, and we would build mountainous castles out of wet sand, letting it dribble between our fingers into spiring stalagmites. In the evenings, our parents would take us to Gilligan's Island, the rinky-dink amusement park that was about a mile down the boardwalk. We would ride the Ferris wheel, our arms pulled up into the sleeves of our T-shirts to shield from the cold ocean air, the gondola creaking in the wind, and we would stare out across the bay at the bright lights of Atlantic City twinkling in the night like some wonderful dream. Somewhere, there is a photograph of the three of us— me, Toby, and Luke—eight or nine years old, our chests pumped out, beach towels tied around our necks like capes. I haven't been to the ocean in years, but I still love the feeling of running barefoot across hot sand, and when I write to Toby, that's what I try to write about.

During the weekend of the funeral, my parents and I stayed with my grandmother. The four of us hardly spoke to one another, but the house was filled with the sound of worried sighs and rustling newspaper. Toby and his family had lived in a suburb of Pittsburgh, and the story was printed on the front page of every local paper. It ran in the side columns under headlines that used words like *tragedy, massacre, nightmare.* I read over each article carefully, the details throbbing in my imagination: Neighbors had heard screaming. Police found Toby kneeling in the grass in the backyard, his arms and chest covered in blood. An eight-inch kitchen knife was discovered on the back porch. The police reported that Toby had been in a state of psychosis, that he had not responded when they said his name, could not answer when they asked if he knew where he was. My cousin Luke, my Great Aunt Sheryl, and my Great Uncle Rick were all found dead inside the house. Their wounds showed evidence of what the police described as "a very significant struggle."

When I get out of here, Toby writes, *I want to start a band. Another guy here has a stereo in his cell. Sometimes, I go over and listen to music. He doesn't have many CDs, so we always just listen to the same ones, over and over. My favorite is the Pixies. Have you heard of them? I want to start a band that sounds like that. I used to have a guitar. I wasn't very good, but I think I know enough to be able to write songs. I want to write songs about my parents and my brother, so that everyone knows how much I love them.*

By the time I was eleven or twelve years old, my mom had started working as a history professor. Labor Day fell right at the beginning of the fall semester, and so my family stopped making our annual trips to Ocean City. I didn't keep in touch with Toby or Luke at all after that, but I would hear about them when we visited our grandmother at Christmas.

After the funeral, I used to stay awake at night, staring at the ceiling, trying to remember everything that I knew about them. I remembered how the last time that we visited Ocean City, Toby had been grounded. The day before we got there, he'd been shooting fireworks in the street, had aimed a bottle rocket right at the door of this corner store and nearly hit a pair of exiting customers. Giggling, his brother Luke had told me about how the owner of the place came out and shook Toby by the arm, demanding to know where his parents lived.

I remembered little snippets of news that I must have heard from family members in the years after. When I was a teenager, my dad told me about how Toby had been expelled from school. He'd gotten into a fight and had put the other kid in the hospital. I have it in my head that Toby had been sticking up for his brother somehow, but I don't know if that's true or if it's just some explanation that I've made up on my own. Maybe I just want to believe that Toby has done some good in his life.

When I was in college, my grandmother told us that Toby had been diagnosed with schizophrenia. He'd been getting into drugs, too, and my Great Uncle Rick saw that as the real reason for whatever problems Toby was having. That was the last I could remember hearing about any of them until four or five years later, when I sat down in the teachers' lounge to return my dad's phone call.

Toby's letters are usually short, no more than a page, scrawled on the back of prison paperwork—misconduct citations or inmate discipline policy forms. His handwriting is terrible, all cracked-glass angles and sentences that seem to shake their way toward the edge of the page. Once, I went to the library and flipped through a couple of books on graphology—the study of handwriting. Depending on certain patterns in a person's handwriting—like the size of the letters or the amount of space between them—you're supposed to be able to identify different attributes of their personality, their mental well-being, or emotional state. Words that descend across the page rather than running in a straight line are supposed to indicate depression. Inconsistent slants in the stems of letters are supposedly indicative of psychosis. I checked out a few of those books, but after a couple of days, I stopped reading because I was picking out so many things in

Toby's writing. Whenever I write to Toby, rather than scribbling out my own tiny, bow-legged letters, I type and print every page.

In most of my letters, I ask Toby to tell me about his life, to tell me about what he does each day, what sorts of things he enjoys. He tells me about the fights, the gangs. He tells me about listening to music out in the prison yard. He tells me little jokes that he makes up, stories that he thinks are funny, but which mostly strike me as sad. *There's a female guard here named Agata*, he wrote. *We joke that her last name is Fuck You, cause she's so mean. But also she's the only woman here, so every morning, everyone says, Hi, Agata Fuck You.* Other times, when it's obvious that he's not doing well, the jokes are less straightforward, their punchlines nonsensical, absurd. Once, he sent a letter that consisted of just two sentences scribbled across an entire page: *What do you call a school bus covered in fur? A pregnant rat.*

In my last letter, I asked Toby if there were any books that he wanted to read. *Maybe I could send them, if I come across any copies*, I wrote. In his reply, the only book he asked for was the Vulgate—an untranslated Latin version of the Bible. He had never made any mention of religion in his previous letters, and from what I know, my Great Uncle Rick and Great Aunt Sheryl had never taken him or Luke to church. I wrote him back, letting him know that I would keep an eye out.

I followed the news about Toby's trial for months after the funeral. During the trial, he was held at a state hospital for the violently insane. The lawyer that had been appointed to him argued that Toby had a documented history of mental illness and that, at the time of the murders, he had been suffering from a psychotic episode and did not understand what he was doing. A Pittsburgh local news site ran a clip that showed him being led from the courtroom, shackled at the wrists and ankles. He was dressed in baggy hospital scrubs. His hair was thick and shaggy, his face bearded. He looked nothing like the boy that I picture when I think of him. His movements were slow, sedated. "I'm sorry," he said as he walked past the camera, and his voice was flat, emotionless. He stared at his feet and you could hear the chains around him jingling. "I miss my parents and I'm sorry."

Once the trial slowed down and the newspapers stopped running stories, it became easier to forget about everything. My wife and I got comfortable in a new apartment. At school, I taught my students *Lord of the Flies* and *Hamlet*. I spoke with my father on the phone every few weeks, but neither of us mentioned Toby. Neither of us mentioned Luke or my Great Aunt Sheryl or my Great Uncle Rick. Once, just before summer break, Mrs. Young stopped me in the hall and asked how I was doing, and for a moment, I had no idea what she was talking about.

"Back in April," she said, "in the lounge. I looked it up in the news. I've been meaning to ask about—"

"Oh," I said, finally understanding. "Yeah. No, I'm fine." I smiled at her. "I'm fine. Thanks."

When I got home after work that day, I typed Toby's name into a search engine and re-read the months-old news stories that came up, scrolling down past the end of each article as if there might be some new detail that I'd missed before. I should have known better than to even glance at the comments sections. *No such thing as mental illness*, one woman wrote, *only God's punishment for sins.* And a little further down, someone else: *I'd love to see that kid try coming into my house with a knife. These kinds of stories are why I bought my AK.*

That night, in bed, in the dark, I wept for the first time, like a child, in my wife's arms.

This past January, Toby wrote asking if I could look up a list of names. They were friends he remembered from high school. He wanted me to find them on Facebook, message them and ask for their addresses so that he could write them too. I carried that letter in my backpack for a month before I finally replied. *I'm sorry,* I wrote. *I've thought about it and the fact is that I don't know what relationship any of these people had to your brother or your parents. I don't know what feelings they might have about you. I know that you are alone, but I can't put someone else in that position. I hope you can forgive me.*

Toby's trial went on for a year before the jury found him guilty on all three counts of first-degree murder. A person's mental illness, they argued, does not preclude him from knowing between right and wrong, nor does it force him to act upon psychotic impulses. Given evidence of how long the struggle with his family must have lasted, the jury believed it was unlikely that Toby was completely unaware of what he was doing. About one week after the decision was made, the prosecuting attorney announced that he would be pursuing the death penalty, and that was when I first wrote to Toby.

A prisoner was killed today, Toby writes. *He was crazy. Everybody hated him. He was always calling everyone faggots and being annoying. A couple days ago, he was messing around in the shower and tried to kiss this guy. He snuck up on his tip-toes and tried to kiss him on the cheek. The guy shoved him away and everyone thought it was pretty funny. This morning, the guy he'd tried to kiss came over to his cell and stabbed him in the neck. He went out on a stretcher with a sheet pulled over him, so we all knew he was dead. The guards took the other guy away and he's been in solitary since.*

Sometimes, I dream of prison riots. In the dream, I'm looking out of a barred window at the gray, rainy beach. The low crescendo of a storm siren is rising all around, and behind me, just over my shoulder, I know that men are being killed. Their faces smashed against the concrete. Carved blades punched into their flesh. The wet sound of clubs coming down against their bruised-fruit skulls. But all of this is horror that I can only imagine; I don't turn around. At some point, I hear Toby moving around in the cell behind me. I don't see him, but I know he's there, and I don't know which of us it is that suddenly says, "Come on, let's get out of here."

At the funeral, all three of the caskets were open. My cousin Luke, my Great Uncle Rick, my Great Aunt Sheryl. Their hands and faces were covered with makeup, caked on so thick that they looked like wax sculptures. I imagined scratching at it with my fingernail, like a lottery ticket, scraping away the layers to find them breathing and sleeping underneath. I wondered later if the makeup must have been applied so thick in order to hide their wounds.

The service took place at a Catholic church next to the cemetery. Organ pipes rose to the ceiling and stained glass windows lined both sides of the nave. A dark red carpet stretched down the aisle and up the steps of the pulpit, and after the priest delivered an opening prayer, several people went to the podium, one at a time, to deliver eulogies. Young men who had been friends of Luke, old men who had been friends of Rick and Sheryl. My Great Uncle Steven stood up and tried to speak. "I can't tell you all what this is like," he said. He stood there a moment, scratching his beard, leaning over the podium. "My brother Rick," he started, but his voice was seized with tears. "My brother Rick," he tried again. He took a step back, covered his eyes with his hand, and stood there until his son rose from the pews and led him back down to his seat.

Toward the end of the service, my father went to the stage. "It's so good to see everyone," he said. "I wish it was under better circumstances." He gripped the podium on either side, as if to hold it steady, like the wheel of a ship. "My Uncle Rick," he said "was one of the smartest, funniest people I've ever known. Though, after they got married, my Aunt Sheryl might've stolen that title from him. I always looked up to them. When I married my wife, I always looked to Rick and Sheryl as role models for the kind of marriage that I wanted to work toward. I'm going to miss them, and I'm going to miss Luke. It's terrible to lose anyone this way, but I'm going to do my best to remember them as the wonderful people that they were." He took a deep breath, stared out at the silent crowd. "None of us has mentioned Toby yet," he said, "and I understand how difficult it is to think of him now. But I think it's important that we remember him too. I won't say anything more about him, but we shouldn't forget him either."

Everyone gathered in a small reception hall at the cemetery's funeral home. There was wine, bottled water, cold cut sandwiches with toothpicks plunged through their centers. I found myself standing in a circle with some men about my age who had been friends with Luke. They traded half-smiles and shared stories about when they'd all been in high school together. A few of them had tears coming down their cheeks, had voices punctuated with sobs, but none of this stopped them from laughing with each other. Someone passed around a bottle of Irish whiskey and when it came our way, we each poured shots into plastic cups. "To Luke," one of them said, and we drank.

Does anyone else from our family write to you? I asked Toby in one letter.

Only you and your dad, he responded. *But he hasn't written since I was in the hospital. I haven't heard from him in a long time.*

Toward the end of the reception, my father and I stepped outside, into the parking lot. The weather was cold, but we needed some fresh air.

"Hey," someone shouted, and we turned to see my Great Uncle Steven walking across the parking lot toward us. "Been looking for you," he said. He walked up to my dad.

"How are you holding up?" my dad asked him.

Steven shook his head. I could smell liquor on his breath. "What the fuck was that about?" he said. "You think anyone wants to hear that kid's name right now?"

My dad looked back toward the funeral home. People were mingling by the doors, neighbors and more distant relatives rounding up their parties and preparing to leave. "I didn't mean to hurt anyone," my dad said.

"Yeah," Steven said, "well, maybe you're forgetting about Rick. That's my brother in that fucking box in there. That's my brother and his wife. And his boy."

"Steven," my dad said, "Listen, I didn't mean anything by it. I'm sorry."

"You're sorry," Steven said. He looked down at the ground, scraped the toe of his shoe back and forth in the gravel. Then he stepped forward, grabbed my dad by the shoulders of his jacket, shoved him up against a car. Steven raised his fist and when my dad turned his head in anticipation of the blow, his glasses slipped from his face and landed in the gravel at his feet. Steven shoved my dad aside and brought his fist down on the hood of the car instead. My dad stumbled backward. I picked up his glasses. By the time we had collected ourselves, Steven was gone, shuffling out into the parking lot and the hard red light of the evening.

Last year, around the holidays, I wrote to Toby, wishing him a Merry Christmas and asking if he had any resolutions for the new year. When he responded, he didn't acknowledge the question, didn't acknowledge any of my questions. He told me about the nicknames he and the other inmates had given to each other: Killer, Slasher, Psycho. I don't blame him for ignoring my questions. I doubt that the guards have decorated their cells. I don't know what resolutions I expect him to make.

About six months after the jury had settled, the judge waved off the prosecutor's call for the death penalty. Instead, Toby was to serve three consecutive sentences of life in prison.

I think that I'm going to get out, he wrote not long after the sentencing. *My lawyers are going to strike a plea and I think that I'm going to be out within the next six months.*

Maybe his lawyer is crazy too, I thought. I carried the letter around in my backpack for a month, trying to figure out the best way to respond. When I did, I wrote about the tiny sand crabs that we used to catch on the beach, how we'd scoop up whole buckets of sand and then sift through till we held one of their tiny jewel bodies in our hands. They'd scurry along the lines in our palms, trying to find a way out. I didn't mention anything about what he had said. I heard later that my great uncle Steven had written to the judge, demanding that Toby never be released.

I call my father now and then, but we don't speak about Toby, and I haven't kept in touch with any of my extended family in almost four years. My wife and I find excuses: we have Christmas with her parents and one of us always has to work over Thanksgiving. I don't know if any of my family—my parents or my grandmother, my aunt and uncle, my cousins, or my Great Uncle Steven—know that I write to Toby. Lately, whenever a letter from him arrives, I let two or three months pass before I reply. I'll carry his letter in my backpack for weeks, tucked inside the back cover of whatever book I'm reading, until the edges of the envelope are worn and soft. I carried one letter around until I had finished my book, and then I took it out and tucked the envelope into the back of a new book, carried it around for another month. Sometimes, Toby will send me two or three letters before I ever reply to just the one. I can't help but wonder, when those letters pile up on the table in the dining room, if I never responded, would he keep writing?

I try to imagine what it will be like years from now. I'm thirty-two. My wife and I want to have kids some day, after we've paid off some of our student loans and have a little bit more income. I imagine writing to Toby then, telling him about our children, telling him about baby teeth and first days of school. And what will he say? Will he still respond with news of prison fights and bloodthirsty guards? I try to imagine when I'm old and Toby is old, when we're both in our sixties or seventies or eighties or nineties, nearing the end of just his first life sentence. What will we write about then? Days pass. Weeks. Leaves fall and snow melts. I carried Toby's last letter around with me for almost six months. But I always write him back, eventually.

ACKNOWLEDGMENTS

There are many people who I owe thanks for helping to shepherd this book into existence.

Most of all, thanks to my family: my mom and dad, my brothers Phil and Ray, and my wife Laura. Each of them, in their own way, has helped me to imagine a life in which I'm able to prioritize this work of making up little stories about imaginary people.

Thanks to Rachel Wilkinson, Tim Maddocks, Gabby Pastorek, Scott Romani, Amanda Boyle, Dan McCloskey, Nate McDonough, and Jake Spears, who, over the years, have been my closest literary counselors, have seen this book grow from its earliest stories, have inspired me with their own work, and have helped to keep my compass pointed in the right direction.

Thanks to my teachers, most of all to Bill Lychack, who has been a mentor, a colleague, a neighbor, and a friend, and without whom I would have grown into a much different (and certainly much worse) writer. And thanks to Phil LaMarche and Arthur Flowers, without whom I would never have started writing in the first place.

Thanks to my dear friends Nina Sabak, Tom Bair, Nick Kasunic, Laura Rohrer, Cameron Barnett, Anna Weber, Tom Roth, Aaron Burch, Katie Booth, Morgan Kayser, Geoff Schiller, and Madeline Phillips, who have all supported my writing in ways that are both big and small, and who have all played important roles within the web of writers that make up my little life.

Thanks to Adam and Jesse at Recess Coffee in Syracuse, NY, and to Amy and Clif at Constellation Coffee in Pittsburgh, PA, for providing the spaces where most of these stories were written.

Thanks to Thao Thai, who selected this story from the Non/Fiction Prize finalists, and to Chris Vanjonack, Kristen Elias Rowley, Becca Bostock, Tara Cyphers, Stuart Rodriguez, Samara Rafert, Olivia Sergent, Jason Gray, Adam Bohannon, and everyone at *The Journal,* Mad Creek Books, and the Ohio State University Press whose labor helped to bring this book into the world. Thanks, also, to Madalina Panaghie, whose art appears on the cover.

Finally, thanks to each of the publications in which these stories first appeared, some in slightly different forms: "The Wrong House" in *Arts & Letters*; "The Storyteller" in *The Baffler*; "The Familiar Dark" in *Confrontation*; "You Have to Talk to Mary Anne" in *december*; "My Prisoner" in *Electric Literature*; "Shit Plate" in *Epiphany*; "Letters from Toby" in *Epoch*; "Lake Shore Limited" in *The Forge Literary Magazine*; "Blindness" and "The Cursed Treasure of the McDaniels Kids" in *Hobart*; "Crime and Punishment" in *The McNeese Review*; "Hand-Me-Downs" in *Redivider*; and "How I Came to See the World" in *Water-Stone Review*.

THE JOURNAL NON/FICTION PRIZE
(formerly The Ohio State University Prize in Short Fiction)